Nanny McPhee Returns

A Warning to the Reader

This is a slightly odd book, being a mixture of story and diary. It is the story of *Nanny McPhee Returns* and the diary of the filming of the story, all mixed up.

I did not write it like this on purpose – it just happened while I was on the film set and seemed an interesting way to do it. If you get bored with the story you can always just read the diary. And vice versa. Good luck.

Also about Nanny McPhee

Nanny McPhee: The Collected Tales of Nurse Matilda
by Christianna Brand • illustrated by Edward Ardizzone

Nanny McPhee Returns

Emma Thompson

BLOOMSBURY

NEW YORK BERLIN LONDON

For Grandpa Eric, Grandma Fifi, Grandpa Dong and Grandma Yonnie
and their grandchildren, Ernie, Gaia, Walter and Tindy

First published in Great Britain in March 2010 by Bloomsbury Publishing Plc
as *Nanny McPhee and the Big Bang*
Published in the United States of America in August 2010
by Bloomsbury Books for Young Readers
www.bloomsburykids.com

For information about permission to reproduce selections from this book, write to
Permissions, Bloomsbury BFYR, 175 Fifth Avenue, New York, New York 10010

Library of Congress Cataloging-in-Publication Data
available upon request
ISBN 978-1-59990-472-6 (paperback) • ISBN 978-1-59990-473-3 (hardcover)

Typeset by Dorchester Typesetting Group Ltd
Printed in the U.S.A. by Worldcolor Fairfield, Pennsylvania
2 4 6 8 10 9 7 5 3 1 (paperback)
2 4 6 8 10 9 7 5 3 1 (hardcover)

All papers used by Bloomsbury Publishing, Inc., are natural, recyclable products
made from wood grown in well-managed forests. The manufacturing processes
conform to the environmental regulations of the country of origin.

The Diary

Here we are on the first day of the shoot of the new Nanny McPhee film. I am playing Nanny McPhee, but not today because she does not appear in this scene. Today I am just the writer. I am here in case anyone needs to change what they say or needs something extra to say or needs to CUT DOWN what they say.

We are on the set of Deep Valley Farm and a most magnificent set it is. Months ago, Susanna White (the Director – see Glossary) and Simon Elliott (the Designer – see Glossary) saw this location and decided it was perfect for the story. So Simon drew lots of pictures and hundreds of people worked like stink and now I am sitting in front of a beautiful old farmhouse with a dovecote and outhouses, an original ancient barn and a fascinating garden, which ALL looks as if it has been here for hundreds of years but in fact was only finished last Thursday.

I'm wearing mud-covered snow boots, leggings (ill-advised) and an enormous puffy jacket. I am sitting next to my friend Lindsay Doran, who is producing the film (see Glossary). To our right is the Scratch-O-Matic (see page 17); to my left, the Sound Department (see Glossary). It's raining and we have had to stop filming.

'Why is it raining?' I whine to Lindsay.

'Because we are shooting this picture in England during the summer,' says Lindsay. 'Of course it's raining.'

Lindsay has produced lots of films in England during the summer and, even though she is American, she understands our weather. Everyone is squelching about, looking depressed, especially Mike Eley, the DP (see– you get the idea).

You're in the way!

Lady Carrington, I mean, of course, their servants — but you knew that), and took them along, hoping to find them husbands.

Prunella knew exactly what was expected of her. She made a beeline for the richest young lord present and pretended to like everything he liked, even though she wasn't remotely interested in war machines or maps of seventeenth-century Europe.

Isabel, however, spotted a rather lovely meadow beyond the grounds of the palace where the party was taking place and decided to go and look for moles. Leaving her enormous bonnet under a hydrangea, she hitched up her posh frock and climbed over the wall.

It was a pretty day and Isabel was looking very pretty in it. So when a young farmer by the name of Rory Green came by in his pony and trap and saw her, he fell instantly in love. Impulsive by nature (as anyone who knows anything about the world would already have realised, and, quite frankly, it's pretty stupid to fall in love with a pretty girl in a pretty frock in a pretty field on a pretty day. Don't. Find out what she's like first), he parked the pony and leapt into the field to say hello. The fact is that Isabel was also quite impulsive and, upon seeing the handsome young man leaping over the gate and hailing her with quite the nicest smile she'd ever seen, she went and fell instantly in love too.

A recipe for disaster, I hear you cry, and under less fortunate circumstances you would be perfectly right. But as luck would have it, Isabel and Rory were not only impulsive but really enjoyed the same things. Things like egg and cress, spiders' webs after rain, the smell of cow parsley and, surprisingly, early thatching techniques. They realised very quickly that they simply had to get married and have babies together.

Well.

You can imagine the reaction.

Poor Prunella, who'd done so well and got engaged to someone she'd soon end up loathing, was completely ignored as Lord and Lady Carrington tried to persuade Isabel that she was delusional and needed six months in a Belgian sanatorium to cure her of her fantasies. There was a lot of sputtering and muttering and cold baths and doctor's recommendations until finally Isabel got so cheesed off that she packed a small bag and eloped.

Eloping doesn't much happen any more, but it must have been great fun. What happened was this: you decided you wanted to marry someone, your family all said 'no' and threatened to lock you up, upon which you crept out in the middle of the night, got into a pony and trap and galloped to Gretna Green, which is the first bit of Scotland, where you were married by the blacksmith! How exciting is that? What's more, afterwards the blacksmith re-shod your pony for the journey home.

So that's what Isabel and Rory did, and of course Lord and Lady Carrington were very cross and, much as you might expect, went and cut her off without a penny.

The Diary

It's not raining any more but it is rather damp and cold. I am very jealous of Rory and Isabel in their sunny field. Why is the weather always so much better in stories? One of our Other Important Producers (see Glossary) has come to check and see we're all managing. He's called Eric and is sometimes very nice to us.

'Very nice' meaning that if he thinks we are doing

well he says supportive things like 'It all looks fantastic' and 'I can't believe that's not real mud' and 'Well done' and 'Carry on'. But if he thinks we are not doing well he doesn't say any of that but stomps about looking fierce and saying things like 'Why haven't you finished that bit?' and 'Hurry up'. It's all right. That's his job.

refreshing the mud

We are on our fifth Set-Up (see Glossary) and it's only 11.30. That's not bad going for the first day. Plus, it's not a normal first day. It's a first day featuring five children, a cow, some chickens, a goat, two feet of mud every-where you go, three cameras and 140 crew people.

Even Steven Spielberg would go a bit green at the thought. Susanna's eyes are twinkling even more than usual.

We are all covered with mud from head to toe. But  it's not real mud so it doesn't feel the same. It's just as much fun and less smelly. It's made of sand and water and some chemical beginning with *B* – wait, let me ask one of the Art Department . . . Bentonite, apparently. That means it doesn't dry up like normal mud. It also means that unlike normal mud, it's quite scratchy to touch. It makes the most wonderful squelching noises when you walk in it and there is a prize offered for the first person to slip over properly.

You will, by the way, be appalled to hear that the real Nanny McPhee story hasn't even started yet. The bit I've just told you happened before this story starts. But I think it's good to know a little about someone's family, and Isabel is the mum in our story so she's very important.

You're in the way!

I am sitting on a pile of hay.

I am in the Camera Department's way.

10

Emma, the Camera Loader (see Glossary) for 'A' camera, has just asked Russ, the Focus-Puller (see Glossary), this question:

'What was your last T-stop?'

I don't know what she's talking about. But I know it's not about stopping for tea.

Anyway. Where were we? Oh yes.

The Story

Isabel and Rory were married by the blacksmith, moved into Rory's farm, and had three children called Norman, Megsie and Vincent. They were about to live happily ever after when a war broke out.

This, I regret to tell you, is typical of Real Life.

Just when you think everything's fine and dandy, something happens and you have to ADAPT.

Adapting is not as much fun as eloping, although it can be character-building.

It certainly was for Isabel, Norman, Megsie and Vincent. Poor Rory Green had to go off in an itchy uniform not quite knowing where and not quite knowing when – or even if – he'd be back. It was ghastly.

The night before he left, Isabel (or Mrs Green as I'll call her from now on) cooked his favourite meal. It was fried cheese, which is cheddar grated on to a tin plate, grilled till it's melted, with a bit of vinegar or Worcestershire sauce tipped in and eaten with a heel of bread. The cheese always burns a little at the edges and these you *must* scrape off with a blunt knife and save until last because they are the best bits.

No one was very hungry.

They all scraped off their burnty bits and gave them to Mr Green. He ate them up and smiled and smiled, which was good of him because he was the least hungry of them all and actually felt more like crying than smiling.

'Don't forget to scratch the piglets,' he said cheerily.

Ah.

Not the sort of thing you hear every day. Or maybe you do, what do *I* know? You might have the sort of dad who says things like 'Don't forget to scratch the piglets/cows/goats/

elephants' all the time. Lucky you.

At any rate, it gives me the chance to tell you a bit more about Mr Green before he goes off because you might as well know exactly who you're missing.

I expect you remember he's handsome, impulsive and has the nicest smile ever. Unlike Mrs Green, he was born to parents who understood each other quite well and were very happy as a result. They were farmers and had two boys, Rory and Phil. As I keep telling you, families are weird. In spite of all their parents' niceness, Rory and Phil were very different kettles of fish. Rory was kind, loving and imaginative. He could mend virtually anything and felt all sorts of things in his bones that turned out to be true, like when one of the new-born lambs was in trouble or when the cow slid into the river by mistake. Phil, on the other hand, was lazy, nervous and ambitious. He had no discernible talent for anything. Nobody's fault, that's just how he was. As a result, he was jealous of his brother and very keen to do things like put salt in his porridge, marmalade in his wellies and frogs in his bed.

Mr and Mrs Green worried about Phil's behaviour but were too busy on their farm to find ways of helping him to change. So he was just left as he was.

The Diary

There is a cow in our story called Geraldine. She is being played by a film cow whose name is Beryl. She arrived

I'm not coming out in that – I've just had my hoofs done!

on set an hour ago, took a violent dislike to the pretend mud and refused to leave her trailer. This is why they tell you never to work with animals. They are unpredictable. Also, one of my jackdaws has been naughty. In our film there is a jackdaw called Mr Edelweiss. Some of his bits will be computer-generated but a lot of his acting will be done by real jackdaws. The Animal Trainers (see you-know-what) and I have been working with three different birds for six weeks already. They are called Devil, Al and Dorian. It is Devil who has been naughty. Last night he caught a mouse (which wasn't naughty) and ate it (which was). It means that overnight he put on 8 grams in weight which means that he can't be fed today and consequently can't work because he will only work for food. I had no idea jackdaws were such finely tuned instruments. Apparently if they eat too much they can't fly or they explode or something.

Martin Harrison is our First Assistant Director (see Glossary) and, apart from the Director, is really the most important person on the set. He's just come up to me and said that when he first read the script he thought to himself, Oh, what a lovely simple story. He now realises that the lovely simple story is without a doubt the most complicated film he's ever worked on. This is largely due to the preponderance of animals and children and also goes to prove once again that simple is never easy.

I am watching Oscar Steer, who, aged six, is our youngest actor apart from the piglets, who are only a month old. He is so clever and funny. He can even run in the mud.

The Story

So now you know a bit about Phil and Rory. There's just one other important thing I have to tell you. Rory adored his children and would spend hours making things for them. The best thing he'd ever made was a machine called the Scratch-O-Matic. He'd had the idea one long summer's day as he was watching Vincent scratching the piglets with the end of a broom. Piglets love being scratched and they would jostle each other for position under Vinnie's broom handle. Vinnie would try and scratch each piglet equally but inevitably the strongest ones would get the most attention and then it would be suppertime and Vinnie would have to go indoors complaining that the littlest piggies had been left out. Mr Green sat up all night with a huge bit of paper and a pencil, then spent an entire day in the barn sawing and hammering and occasionally letting out great bellows of rage when something had gone wrong with his calculations. Then he came in and went to sleep so soundly in front of the fire

that Mrs Green just left him there for the night. In the morning, he was up and about before anyone, and when the rest of the family had come downstairs for breakfast, he proudly announced that he had something special to show them all. Consumed with curiosity, the

Scratch-O-Matic

children and Mrs Green followed him into the barn, where a sheet had been flung over a gigantic structure right in front of the pigsty. Pink with pride, Mr Green whipped away the sheet to reveal an amazing machine. It all started with a bicycle seat and pedals. You sat on the seat and pedalled, and all at once a great system of levers and cables whooshed into action. The cables controlled the levers, which controlled a selection of brushes and sticks and broomhandles which all moved about as music came out of a great gramophone horn. Each little pig was settled under a brush and scratched to its heart's content as it listened to whatever music you fancied putting on to the record player, which is an old-fashioned term for a sort of iPod. All the children said the Scratch-O-Matic was the cleverest invention since sliced bread, and Vincent in particular thought it was the finest thing he'd ever seen in his life.

All this just goes to show that Mr Green was dad-tastic and the idea of him having to leave home and go off to fight and maybe even get hurt made them all thoroughly miserable.

On the morning of his departure, everyone saw him up to the top of the lane and waved him off as he disappeared round the corner. They shouted and jumped and made loads of noise. As soon as he'd gone from view everyone fell silent. Mrs Green looked at the three sad faces.

'Come on,' she said. 'Dad'll want something sweet when he comes home so let's make him some strawberry jam. I've saved up sugar specially for it!'

This idea rather cheered the children up, so they went back home, picked strawberries and made a really gorgeous pot of jam for Mr Green's return. Megsie made the frilly top and tied the ribbon and Vincent drew the label with more care than usual. Mrs Green put it in its own special corner of the pantry shelf. Every day from then on, Vincent would go and check to see it was safe and hadn't been eaten by mice.

The Diary

It's Day Two and raining hard. No strawberries here, that's for sure. All the wheels on the cameras and lights get stuck in the mud and we work at least 30 per cent slower than usual. Phil Sindall, our Camera Operator (see Glossary), is sitting on the Dolly (see Glossary) with his forehead resting on the eyepiece. He is meditating while he waits. There is no one who has to be more patient than a Camera Operator, and there is no Camera Operator more patient than Phil. It's a bit like having Buddha on the set.

There's absolutely nothing going on here.

I suppose I'd better just get on with the story.

The Story

The days and weeks went by and were filled with all the usual chores and with Mrs Green's job. She worked at the village shop, which was owned and run by a frantically old lady called Mrs Docherty. It was a lovely shop, full of coloured drawers, and ladders in case you needed anything from 'up top'. In the olden days, Mrs Docherty had colour-coded everything. Lentils went in the orange drawer, knicker elastic in the pink drawer and tap washers in the grey drawer, that sort of thing. But she had forgotten what colour was for what years ago and now everything was jumbled in, higgledy-piggledy. Mrs Green knew the shop inside out though and could always find you exactly what you wanted. She loved Mrs Docherty but had to admit that failing memory and eyesight did render her something of a liability. Mrs Green was apt to find soap snuggled in with oats (which had a slightly carbolic aftertaste as a result) and, on one occasion, rice mixed up with the ball-bearings. It wasn't easy.

All the children wrote lots of letters to their father and so did Mrs Green, and they would normally get a lovely letter back, always from a different place. Once they had even got a letter from Africa, and Mrs Green had said to the children that at least it was nice that their dad was getting to see a bit of the world. But for the past few months, they had written and written and got no reply.

That morning, the postman had come to the door with a letter which caused huge excitement. But it wasn't one of the little blue envelopes they were used to receiving from their father. It was a letter made of thick cream parchment paper, the sort of stuff you don't expect to see except in castles. The writing on it was elegant and sloping and it smelled very faintly of bergamot.

All the children were very curious about it indeed and crowded about Mrs Green as she carefully opened the envelope.

'Oh!' she said, and sat back in her chair, staring at the beautiful paper in perplexity.

'What, what?' said Megsie. 'Can I look?'

Mrs Green handed her the letter and explained to the others that her sister, Prunella (about whom you know so much but Norman, Megsie and Vincent knew next to nothing) was worried about bombs dropping in London and was going to send her two children to stay in the country with the Greens.

It was all very sudden.

Mrs Green was perfectly astonished because after she'd been cut off without a penny, she'd only seen her sister once. Prunella, who was now Lady Gray, had made the journey from London to the farm in a pale blue Rolls-Royce. When she'd arrived she'd been so appalled by the mud in the yard and the presence of grubby animals and germ-ridden poultry that she'd decided simply to roll down her window and chat to Mrs Green from the safety of the Rolls. This, as you can imagine, did not lead to a very intimate or sisterly conversation and, after a very short while, Prunella had rolled up her window again and gone back to London, overcome by what she saw as the squalor of her sister's home. Mrs Green had been equally appalled by the ridiculously expensive car and the fact that Prunella had been wearing a sapphire tiara during the daytime.

She certainly hadn't expected her sister to send her very own children to a place like Deep Valley Farm.

But so it appeared.

Megsie, Norman and Vincent were thrilled. New blood! People to play with! People to share the chores with! Rich people who might have access to chocolate!

'When are they coming, then?' asked Norman, pulling on his wellies, which, as usual, were damp inside. (I hate that.)

'Next Tuesday,' said Mrs Green, doing up Vincent's shoelaces and putting on her coat inside out. 'We'll have to tidy.'

The Diary

I'll stop there for a minute because no one's interested in tidying, for crying out loud. Let them get on with it. It's raining really hard here now. All the children are ready for their close-ups. The poor chickens are sitting in the pretend mud, which is getting thinner and thinner because of the rain. Devil is still too fat to work and Beryl has gone on hunger strike. If it goes on like this we certainly won't survive the next three and a half months.

Jackie Durran, our costume designer, has come to show me my khaki uniform. She is an absolute genius, who wears mad hats and invents all these brilliant things for people to wear, like Mrs Green's costumes, which all remind me of a cottage garden. You'll hear about the khaki uniform later in the story.

But wait! The pattering upon the plastic roof of my

palatial trailer (it has pelmets) has stopped! Chris Stoaling, our Second AD (see Glossary), has knocked and said we're off to shoot the arrival of the Rolls-Royce. Massively exciting. I am going to pull on wellies and rush down there to get in the way.

My wellies, by the way, are never damp inside. That's because my Dresser (see Glossary), Helen Ingham, makes sure they are clean and toasty every day. Only the actors are cared for in this way – everyone else has to wash their own wellies. Helen, or 'H' as she is known, is very funny. We giggle a lot.

Just arrived. Oh, it's started to rain again. Everyone's standing about in the mud looking glum. We're not shooting the arrival of the Rolls-Royce. Massively boring. Better get on with the story then. There's nothing else to do . . .

Might call this bit Chapter Two. Why not? It has a nice ring to it.

The Story

Chapter Two. The day before the arrival of the Gray children, everyone got a bit tense. The children had been too excited to sleep and had woken up grumpy as a consequence. Vincent was feeling resentful because Norman had made him promise to wash the bedclothes with Megsie instead of scratching the piglets. He'd been stewing on this for ages and finally decided to do something really naughty and steal Norman's last sweetie from the secret tin.

I had better explain something here; I don't know about you but I wasn't really allowed sweeties when I was little. My dad used to buy us a sixpenny ice-lolly on a summer Sunday but that was pretty much it. Perhaps because of this I wanted and loved sugar in all its forms more than anything else in the world. The situation for the Green children was similar because during the war there was hardly any sugar in the whole country and certainly not enough for people to have sweeties every day. They were allowed about two ounces of sugar a week per family, which is about one bite of a Mars Bar. To share. So you can imagine, after a few months of that, the very thought of a sweetie would just about drive you mad with desire. So mad that you might consider stealing someone's last one, especially if you were cross with the person to whom it belonged. Vincent was *very* cross with Norman, so he crept into the best parlour, climbed up on to the dresser, took the secret tin down and opened it. There, at the bottom, was the last sweetie. A lemon drop. Not, you might think, the most exciting sweetie in the world, but for all the reasons I have just mentioned, the thing that Vincent wanted more than life itself. He took it out, replaced the tin, got down from the dresser and then made his one mistake. A fatal mistake. He decided to open the sweetie there and then. As any fool knows, all children can hear the rustling of sweetie paper from a distance of several miles. This applies even if children get regular supplies and aren't in the deprived condition of the Greens. So the moment Vincent started to unwrap the lemon drop, Megsie, who was outside milking Geraldine, heard, dropped the milk bucket and raced inside. Norman was oiling the tractor in the barn and, despite being several hundred metres away from the wrapper *and* whistling to himself, heard as well and headed straight for the best parlour, roaring, 'Who's eating my last sweetie?!'

Vincent only just had time for a few good sucks on the lemon drop before his siblings burst in on him and, at a glance, worked out what he'd been up to.

A passionate brawl ensued. Megsie got hold of Vincent and turned him upside down in the hope of shaking the sweet out. When this didn't work, Norman tried to prise open his brother's jaws but got bitten for his pains. Vincent sucked harder and harder as Norman yelled, 'That was MINE!' over and over again.

Suddenly an appalled Mrs Green rushed in.

'Stop it! Stop it at once!' she yelled. 'Stop fighting! Stop shouting! Get off the furniture!!'

Mrs Green was furious. She'd spent hours trying to get the best parlour tidy just in case her sister turned up with the cousins. By the time Mrs Green had got the children to stop fighting and stop shouting, Vincent had finished the lemon drop.

'Look here,' said Mrs Green crossly, 'you lot are supposed to be getting the farm spick and span for the cousins and all you're doing is fighting, fighting, fighting, when what I want to be seeing is sharing, sharing, sharing!'

The children groaned.

'We're not sharing Dad's jam with the cousins!' said Vincent defiantly.

'No, of course not, silly,' said Mrs Green. 'That's for Dad when he comes home! I mean your beds and your toys and everything.'

'When is he coming home?' said Vincent.

Everyone went quiet. This was the question no one else dared to breathe. The sad fact was that not only had Mr Green not replied to their letters, but he had also missed his last leave and there had been no word from him or from anyone to explain why. When Mrs Green had tried to contact his unit there had been a lot of

official language about 'troop movements' and 'belated leave' but no hard information about exactly where Mr Green might be or when he might be coming home. Like all very scary topics, it was something the family didn't talk about much in case something or other came true. But Vincent was only five and sometimes he forgot the rules.

'I don't know, darling,' said Mrs Green, suddenly calm and quiet.

'Why won't he reply to my letter? His last one came years ago!' said Vincent, wandering over to look at the tied-up little bundle of

letters that was kept safe on
the mantelpiece.

'Three months, darling,
that's all,' said Mrs Green.

'Yes, but why? Why won't he reply?'

'They move them around a lot, that's all it is.
Your letter's sitting somewhere safe waiting for
the next post, darling –'

Vincent persisted. 'How do we know something bad hasn't happened to him?'

'Well –' Mrs Green started to say, but Megsie
interrupted.

'Because they always send a telegram when
something bad's happened. They're little yellow
envelopes –'

'I know!' said Vincent. 'I've seen one. It came
for this boy at school. It said his brother was
dead.'

'That's quite enough, all of you!' said Mrs
Green sternly. 'You are quite right, Megsie, and
that's a very sad story, Vinnie, but nothing like
that is going to happen!'

Mrs Green didn't mean to be stern, but she
was awfully scared about her husband and what
might have happened to him and the only way

she could cope with the fear was by being absolutely sure and certain that Mr Green would one day be walking back over the hill to them all.

'And now I really have got to go to work. Please get on with all the chores and don't eat the last bit of ham till I've cut it up evenly otherwise there will be arguments.' And even though Mrs Green knew she hadn't managed the situation terribly well she had to leave, so with one last glance at the three sad faces, she rushed out of the door.

The children didn't feel like fighting any more. Norman, still grumpy about the sweetie and as concerned about his father as the rest of them, went off without a word to do his chores.

Megsie followed, and Vincent, having already had a bashing from both his siblings, decided that he might as well continue to be naughty, so instead of helping wash the bedclothes as he had been told, he went into the barn and started to pedal the Scratch-O-Matic. No sooner had all the piglets settled under their favourite scritcher for a good going-over than Norman marched in, hauled Vincent off and screeched, 'You are in Big Trouble!'

Vincent wrenched himself out of Norman's grasp and raced out of the barn. Norman followed at speed, only to be tripped up by Vincent with Megsie's broom which she'd just mended and which broke again as Vincent and Norman careered into a huge heap of dung she'd just finished sweeping, which collapsed and scattered over the yard, by which time everyone was furious all over again. They were chasing each other about and screaming when suddenly Megsie saw something and stopped.

'LOOK!' she yelled.

No one took any notice.

'LOOK, LOOK!' she yelled again, and this time Vincent turned and saw an extraordinary sight. A huge motor car was coming up the lane. You, I imagine, are quite accustomed to seeing lots of cars every day of the week, but these children had hardly ever even seen ONE, let alone one like this. It was enormous and shiny and two different colours and had a silver lady statuette on the bonnet.

The Diary

Freezing today. For some reason May has decided to be January. We're all wearing four layers and fur hats. Well, I am. Poor Danny Mays, who is playing the chauffeur Blenkinsop, has to do a backward roll in the mud and fall into the  duck pond. He's got a wetsuit on under his uniform but still . . . No one told him he was going to be performing stunts, and he's being brilliant and excited about it and making us all laugh.

At least it's not DARK and not raining. I see we've got to quite an exciting part of the story so let's go back to it. There's nothing much going on here. Lots of people standing about while other people push lamps through the mud, swearing quietly. I'm sitting in a patch of nettles but at least I'm not in the way . . . oh wait! Something happened! Oscar slipped over in the mud! He wins the prize and it's TEN POUNDS. Now everyone is *trying* to slip over in the mud so they can win a prize too. But it's too late.

The Story

Yes – the car was two colours! Plum and Cadbury purple! And the chauffeur had a pale grey uniform with a purple stripe down the leg and a peaked cap. The children stared and stared. The Rolls-Royce purred up the lane like a big metal cat, and pulled into the yard. Megsie was the first to realise what had happened.

'It must be the cousins,' she breathed.

'But they're not due until tomorrow,' said Norman.

All three of them raced up to meet the magnificent vehicle as it pulled up by the farm-house. Vincent was so awed that he couldn't close his mouth. He just stood there like a gold-fish, staring. They all expected – well, I'm not sure what they expected – the cousins to jump out, shouting 'Hello!' and 'I'm So-and-so!' or 'We've brought presents from London!' or, even

more likely, 'Where's your loo?' – all the normal things that people say after a long journey. But there was a deathly silence from the car. Only the chauffeur, his face set like stone, hopped quickly out (straight into the mud) and opened the passenger door, standing smartly by it like a soldier. As the door opened they all heard a strange, high, shrieking noise. Vincent went to look in at the window and the shrieking became a sustained scream, which made him jump back in fright.

Norman and Megsie stared as a boy with yellow hair stepped out gingerly. I say 'boy', but he looked far more like a perfect miniature adult. His hair was flaxen (which is another word for yellow) and flopped over his forehead in an 'I've got posh floppy hair' way. He was wearing a yellow check suit, belted at the waist, and proper leather lace-ups. He was also carrying a copy of *The Times* newspaper and a large bar of chocolate, which he was busy munching.

As soon as he clapped eyes on the chocolate, Vincent gasped.

'Is that a Fry's Triple-Layer Chocolate Bar with Cinder Crunch Topping?' he asked breathlessly. There was nothing Vincent didn't know about Fry's chocolate. Before the war he'd got into the habit of saving his pocket money (tuppence a week when times were good, a penny when they weren't – I know it doesn't sound like much but these were the days when a penny would buy you four enormous toffee chews that could prevent speech for hours and once pulled out one of my uncle's molars) and investing in a chocolate bar that he ate immensely slowly, sometimes over a period of several weeks.

The Diary

Raining. Dark. It's summer in England all right. We are doing what is known as weather cover. This is when you are supposed to be shooting something in glorious sunlight or even just plain old daylight and there turns out to be neither of those things available and you have to go indoors and shoot something else. It's a bit like wet playtime. I rehearsed with the jackdaws this morning, which was bliss. They really are very clever. They haven't seen me for a while and yet remember everything. I think it will be possible to shoot most of the scenes with me and one of them in a Two-Shot (see Glossary) and then Pick Up (see Glossary) what we don't get after-wards with Singles (see Glossary). Olly, one of our Props Artists (see Glossary), has just walked by carrying

I never forget a face.

four white Foam Piglets (see Glossary – sorry, lots of Glossary, but there we are). Not a sight you see very often. The chickens have proved a little disappointing today. Instead of skittering about as the car arrives, they seem to just stand there as if stapled to the ground. The fact is, of course, that they are indeed pegged to a bit of wood, which is then covered with mud to hide it. Prevents them from escaping, see. Oh dear, this weather. Everyone's damp and exuding a warm animal smell. It's like being in a wet stable. Anyway. Back to Cyril and his chocolate bar.

The Story

Vincent, eyes out on chapel-hooks, trotted up to Cyril to get a closer look at the confectionery.

'Since you ask,' drawled Cyril, draping himself elegantly over the shiny bonnet of the Rolls, 'it *is* a Fry's Triple-Layer Chocolate Bar with Cinder Crunch Topping. Would you like some?'

His vocal chords paralysed with desire, Vincent could only nod so hard that his head nearly came off.

'Thought so,' said Cyril, airily popping the last square into his mouth and dropping the empty

wrapper into Vincent's upturned palms.

'Pity there's none left,' he added, sauntering round to look at Megsie and Norman, who had been watching the exchange with horror.

'That was rotten,' hissed Megsie, and, let's face it, she was right.

I suppose I'd better explain a little bit about Celia and Cyril before you begin to hate them too much. What you have to bear in mind is that their parents were useless. Lord Gray (the person Prunella had made the beeline for at the Garden Party) was always being Very Important in the War Office and had never once been a normal dad at home. He'd also never recovered from being detested by his wife and had taken refuge in work virtually day and night. He even had a little camp bed in a broom cupboard at the War Office, which he slept in whenever he couldn't face being ignored in his own home. Prunella we know too well already. Disgusted by her choice of husband, she spent her days making purchase after purchase in London's most expensive shops. She was so well known to the staff at Harrods that red carpet was laid down for her entrances and exits and champagne served upon her arrival in each department. Only the really top staff were allowed to look at her. Everyone else had to keep their eyes lowered and remain silent unless addressed. Poor woman. She really hadn't turned out well at all.

As for being a mother – you can imagine what a disaster *that* was.

This was a woman who changed her outfit five times a day, thus:

Breakfast – silken flowing robes, matching turbans and monogrammed slippers.

Elevenses – brocaded jackets and skirts, jaunty little hats with feather trim.

Lunch – exquisitely tailored

suits with matching coats, shoes, gloves and handbags.

Afternoon tea – tea gowns in taffeta and tulle, delicately stitched soft shoes in complementary shades and feather fascinators in her hair.

Dinner – long evening dress with train, vast rubies or diamonds or sapphires, high heels encrusted with precious stones, and tiaras or ostrich-feather head-dresses and velvet capes that flowed around her like water.

Stains were simply not an option.

Babyhood, as you may remember, is a pretty stain-heavy phase of life. Poor Celia had the great misfortune to be brought one morning to her mother by the nurse, just for a brief visit. Lady Gray was in a coffee gown and little Celia in a delightful concoction of rosy ruffles and frills. As Lady Gray raised up the gurgling babe, Celia threw up in spectacular fashion, liberally spattering her mother and several nearby attendants. As a result, Lady Gray refused to touch her until she was seven. This probably accounts for Celia's difficult character. Cyril was sent to boarding school when he was two and a half and only saw his parents fleetingly on school holidays when there was some sort of 'do' and both children had to be dressed up in scratchy clothes and wheeled out for inspection by a lot of grand people they didn't know. Cyril called his father 'sir' and, as far as he knew, had never been kissed or hugged by either parent or anyone else, for that matter. So. Have a little sympathy.

The Diary

Weather-cover scenes triumphant. Asa Butterfield, who plays Norman, and Eros Vlahos, who plays Cyril, acted wonderfully. Asa has been in lots of other things, like *The Boy in the Striped Pyjamas* and stuff, so he's used to filming. Eros is a stand-up comic – he writes his own material and performs it in places, like at the Edinburgh Festival. He's fourteen. I am amazed. They are both extraordinary. All the crew are very impressed. Beryl the cow is back on set with her giant googly eyes and psychological issues. I'm in what we call 'stage three nose' (large) but no warts. We're hoping to get a shot of

me in silhouette tonight. After eleven hours in the damp, I feel as though I'm covered with a very fine layer of mould. Horrid. And possibly true. Such a good day though. Home to eat lemon meringue pie for Greg's (see Glossary) forty-third birthday. I met him when he was twenty-eight. Good grief.

The Story

There stood Cyril, watching as the chauffeur, whose name was Blenkinsop, got into an increasingly violent struggle with Celia, who was refusing, absolutely, to get out of the car. She clung to the luxury interior as a drowning person clings to a lifebelt, screeching all the while:

'No! No, Blenkinsop! Take me home! Take me away from here!! It's not nice!'

'Let go of the drinks cabinet, Miss Celia,' pleaded the hapless Blenkinsop, who might have had a very smart chauffeur's uniform but was paid very little for driving the Grays around whenever they wanted and wherever they wanted at all times of the day and night.

Finally, of course, Celia did let go, and without any warning, with the result that poor Blenkinsop went careering over his own shoulders into the duck pond. Meanwhile, Norman and Cyril had been exchanging insults and enraging each other to such a degree that the inevitable occurred – Norman rushed at Cyril, who bought himself some time by grabbing Celia's boxes of new clothes and throwing them at him. The boxes opened and broke, spilling all the exquisitely fashionable items into the mud, which then got ground in by Megsie and Vincent running after Norman and Cyril to join in with the fun. Seeing this, Celia's screams doubled, startling a flock of pigeons several miles to the west.

'No! Not my Chanel tea gown and matching slippers!' she shrieked. 'Not my Lucien Lelong silk jersey pyjama pants and wrapper!'

She picked up each bedraggled article and gnashed her teeth and yelled, finally running after the others screaming, 'I'll kill you for this!'

Blenkinsop, finding himself briefly alone, decided to make his escape. Just as he was lowering his dung-smeared rear on to the pristine leather of the driver's seat, all the children came roaring around the side of the barn, slapping at each other. Blenkinsop started the engine.

'NOOOOOOOO!!!' screeched Celia, so loudly that everyone had to stop and put their fingers in their ears and several people in the nearby village thought it was an air raid and hid under their kitchen tables. Celia ran to the car. Blenkinsop, about to pull away, saw the desperate look in her eyes and stopped.

'Let me go now, miss,' he said gently. 'You know how Her Ladyship will be if I don't get back in time.'

Celia knew.

'Promise me you'll tell her how awful it is here! *Promise* me!! Tell her she has to come back and get me tomorrow!!'

Poor Blenkinsop. He was a kind man and had all sorts of private thoughts about his employers and how they treated their children. But he was a servant and not allowed anything private at all, especially not thoughts. In those days, servants were expected not to have any feelings at all but just to do as they were told and to do it immediately. I expect, because of that, Blenkinsop understood Celia and Cyril rather well. *They* weren't allowed to express their feelings either. So Blenkinsop gave Celia a sad smile and simply said, 'I'll tell her, Miss Celia. I promise.'

And off he drove. The wheels of the Rolls skidded in the mud, thoroughly splattering Celia. As the noise of the engine died away she took in a huge breath. Cyril took evasive action and ran into the house. All the Greens rushed into the barn as Celia let out the biggest yell of all. Even Mrs Green heard it on her headlong rush down the lane to her work.

'What on earth was that?' she said to herself before running on, worrying.

The Diary

The goat is busy eating the set. Even the nettles are courtesy of the Art Department. The Call-Sheet (see Glossary) is plastered with increasingly plaintive sentences in capitals that read: 'PLEASE PLEASE PLEASE DON'T STAND ON THE GRASS OR NETTLES OR FLOWERS OR ANY OF THE GREENERY. IT'S ALL ART DEPARTMENT' and 'ART DEPARTMENT HAVE GROWN

ALL GREENERY FROM SCRATCH SO PLEASE DON'T SPOIL IT!! PLEASE!!! WE BEG YOU!!!!' The goat can't read, or, if it can, has not been given a call-sheet, or, if it has, has eaten it. Today we have the worst possible shooting conditions of all: rain and sun in succession so the light is always changing. Also, we are in the mud and we have all the children, most of the animals and a Rolls-Royce that keeps sliding about. Everyone is pretty cheerful under the circumstances, except me.

I can't write in this WIND. Bloody weather (excuse my French). Damn and blast it all.

The Story

As I was saying, Mrs Green was worrying. Worrying about the cousins and about her darling Rory, worrying about the harvest and about not having any money to pay for the tractor hire, worrying about all sorts of things, none of them pleasant, when all of a sudden a man holding a big brown envelope jumped out in front of her, giving her a fright.

'I wish you wouldn't keep doing that, Phil!' she said.

Phil was Mrs Green's brother-in-law, Rory's brother and the children's uncle.

'Sorry, Izzy,' he said, unctuously. 'Sorry. How's my gorgeous sister-in-law, then, eh? Eh?'

'No,' said Mrs Green, walking past him.

'No? No what?' said Phil, falling into step beside her.

'You know perfectly well what, Phil, so leave it.'

Mrs Green picked up her pace irritably. Phil picked up his pace too and waggled the envelope at her.

'Izzy, listen; listen, Izzy. We need to sell the farm. *You* need to. You don't have the money to pay the tractor hire and without the tractor you'll lose the harvest, and if you lose the harvest the farm will fail, and if the farm fails you and the children will be out on the street –'

This litany of impending doom was cut off by Mrs Green stopping very suddenly, whipping the envelope out of Phil's hands and smacking him with it.

'Stop it, Phil. I won't have this. I've enough on my plate without you making everything sound worse. We *have* got enough to pay for the tractor. Norman's going to sell the piglets to Farmer Macreadie and that'll tide us over till the harvest. If Rory's still not back then, we'll all have to work very, *very* hard, Phil, and that includes you!'

Phil edged away. He'd been edging away from the word 'work' all his life and so far it seemed to have done the trick. He'd never lifted a finger.

'So take your blooming contract and push it up your chimney. I'm not selling.'

'Izzy – have a heart – the farm *is* half mine –'

Oh dear. I suppose I should've told you about that. Yes. The farm belonged equally to Rory and to Phil even though Phil didn't like farming or animals or barley and had never once helped out, even when Rory was called up to serve in the army. (Phil hadn't been called up because he had flat feet, a fact that only served to prove to him that he must be the luckiest man alive.) Phil had been trying for weeks to get Mrs Green to sell the farm. He was desperate. To explain why I'm going to have to let you in on a secret that not a single other person in the story knows.

Phil was a gambler.

He liked nothing more than to dress in a smart suit and walk into a casino as though he were a very rich man with a lot of money to spend. In fact, he only had one suit, which, unbeknownst to him, had stopped being smart quite a number of years previously. Added to which he was very, very bad at gambling and nearly always lost every penny he had. Like a lot of bad gamblers he always went back, always believed that he would one day win millions and purchase the sky-blue Bentley he had once seen in an advertisement and never stopped desiring.

If Phil had kept his gambling habit to small places in little towns he would probably not be in the mess he was in. But he'd taken the plunge and gone to London one night and only walked into one of the East End's most notorious gambling establishments, a velvet-clad dive called Ruby's, which belonged to a congenitally vicious gangster named Mr Biggles. Mr Biggles had been very successful at evading the law but hadn't entirely managed to evade the army yet. When the call to fight had come, he made a big exit, orchestrating a heroic departure in full uniform at St Pancras railway station, waved off by his weeping family and dozens of fellow gangsters (all secretly thrilled he was going somewhere dangerous), got on to the train and then promptly slipped off it just before Folkestone, where a small plane was waiting to take him to Switzerland. There he spent the rest of the war investing his money in chocolate rabbits and getting unreasonably fat. This was all very unfair on Ruby Biggles, who, astonished by her husband's bravery (which had not heretofore been apparent), genuinely believed he was off fighting the enemy. But she took to gangsterhood like a fish to water and firmly upheld her husband's core principles. They were as follows:

1. Never try to reason with people. Threaten them instead.
2. Never make a threat you don't intend to follow through.
3. Try to make your threats as creative and original as possible. Then they'll really stick in people's minds.
4. Only trust Mr Topsey and Mr Turvey.

This last rule referred to Mr Biggles's henchmen, Vaughn Topsey and Shaun Turvey. They were both *actually* fighting in the war and their places in the organisation had been filled by their daughters, Deirdre and Evelyn. Deirdre Topsey and Evelyn Turvey were both charming in every respect except one: they both really, *really* liked hurting people. They were the perfect sidekicks for Ruby Biggles, who always liked to have everything pleasant about her and insisted that any violence be conducted in locations as far from her person as possible. It wasn't that she was kind or anything; she just didn't like mess.

The Diary

Glory be. The piglets have triumphed. They've galloped down a dappled track, stopped by the apples, started to eat them and got covered by the veil, and they've done it FOUR times perfectly! Then they ran down a sun-drenched hill chased by the children. It's a miracle, in short. David Brown, our Line Producer (see Glossary) is looking all pink he's so happy. 'I can't believe it!' he keeps saying. 'They did it! They did it four times!' Line producers are always very relieved when things go well because they tend to be the first person to get shouted at when things *aren't* going well.

Later: I'm sitting in a field doing a bit of pig-calming. Turns out they're exhausted by all that acting. Baby pig slept in my arms for a full half-hour. Bit whiffy. But very sweet. Anyway, back to Misses Topsey and Turvey and Phil.

The Story

So there was Phil, down in the posh casino pretending he's got money. He took out his pretend pigskin wallet and slapped a five-pound note down on the table. The people around the club looked at him doubtfully. He seemed down at heel but there did appear to be a large wad of banknotes in his hand. This was in fact a chunk of toilet paper cleverly disguised as money. In those days, toilet paper wasn't nice and soft and absorbent but crinkly and hard and shiny like real paper. (There was a cheap brand called Izal which was like wiping your bottom with your homework. I don't want to go into it. It was most unpleasant. I don't think they make it any more.) So Phil didn't have any real money and only had the fiver because he'd nicked it out of Mrs Docherty's till. The game began, and for the first time in his life, Phil won. He kept winning. The next game and the next and the one after that until he was sitting behind a huge pile of chips worth thousands of pounds. Of course they'd let him win. That's what they do. They let you win and win and then they grab it all back at the end with whatever you're wearing thrown in. But Phil didn't know that. He just thought he was the best gambler in the world and that finally the world had found out.

Then another amazing thing happened. For the first time in his life, Phil decided to be sensible. He decided to gather up all his chips and cash them in. They were worth enough – enough to buy him that sky-blue Bentley and drive it about the place until he was sick of it. As he turned from the table, his pockets bulging, he came face to face with a very large woman in a print frock. This, of course, was Mrs Biggles.

'Hello, Mr Green,' she said, smiling at him with enormous and maternal warmth. 'What good luck you've been having!'

Oh, she was smiling and smiling. Phil preened and winked and kissed Mrs Biggles's hand. Then he made to get by her and head for the cashier's desk.

'Where are you going, Mr Green?' said Mrs Biggles, sounding sad.

'Just to cash in my chips,' said Phil.

61

'Why don't you have one last throw?' said Mrs Biggles encouragingly. And she smiled and smiled. Phil, ignoring the tiny note of alarm that had started to go off in his head, thought that he might as well oblige, since she was being so charming and smiling at him so sweetly. Accordingly, and with many winks and grimaces intended to convey his mystery and appeal, he returned to the table and set down a couple of the smaller chips on number nine.

Mrs Biggles's voice cut in from behind.

'Put all Mr Green's chips on number twenty-one, Gervaise.'

Very suddenly, his pockets were roughly emptied and Phil saw the whole evening's winnings being placed on number twenty-one.

'But –' He whirled back to face her. She was still smiling, but somehow Phil knew that she wasn't smiling on the inside. He realised that outright refusal was not an option. So he attempted a compromise:

'It's just that twenty-one isn't my lucky number, that's all,' he said.

'Never mind, Phil,' said Mrs Biggles. 'It's mine.'

Gervaise spun the wheel, the ball landed on

number nine and all Phil's winnings were swept away.

'There, there, Phil,' said Mrs Biggles. 'You're a rich man – have another go.'

Phil was about to explain that he had a bit of a headache and didn't want another go, when more chips were brought over and Mrs Biggles handed them to him.

'I know your word is good, Phil. You don't have to show me your money,' she said sweetly. 'Just put all this on number twenty-one.'

And thus it was that Phil was forced to gamble away money he didn't have. And thus it was that he pledged the family farm to Mrs Biggles and returned to the village with horror in his heart and death at his heels.

The Diary

Goodness only knows what day it is, but I must just tell you about the shenanigans on set. We are dealing with the truncated hours that the children are allowed to work as well as a prosthetic pig diving into the pond and a diver in full scuba gear under the water moving

the pig along so that visual effects can fiddle with the image later, a camera on a Luna crane, water that you can't see in so the diver keeps going in the wrong direction and three children on the bank trying to react to something that isn't there. The whole thing is a nightmare for Martin. I've offered him a cyanide pill. We may have to share it. I adore the results that visual effects give us, and they are a wondrous team, but I hate the methods we have to use to get there. *Ugh.*

Later: I am wet through. This is how it happened.

It was very difficult for the children to act delight and astonishment with nothing to react *to.* So I made a little plot with Martin – the camera started to roll and Martin pulled me bodily off the set and pushed me into the water, where I did quite a lot of very silly things. The children were delighted and astonished, and now that it's in 'The Can' (see Glossary) I am delighted and astonished too.

The Story

Is it Chapter Three yet? I don't know. You decide.

So, if you remember, Phil was desperate to get Mrs Green to sign full ownership of the farm over to him so that he could sign it over to Mrs Biggles.

'Isabel,' he said urgently, 'you haven't even got enough money to pay for this month's tractor hire —'

'Phil,' interrupted Mrs Green, quite rosy with irritation, 'didn't you hear me? Norman has solved that problem by agreeing to sell the piglets to Farmer Macreadie!'

'Sell the piglets to Farmer Macreadie?' said Phil, his eyes narrowing.

'Yes! And that will tide us over to harvest time! Now, if you'll just let me pass —'

But as Mrs Green was about to run off, a voice interrupted. 'Don't panic!' it cried. 'Don't panic! Stop all that panicking! Help is at hand!'

Phil and Mrs Green turned to look as a little round man with round spectacles on a round nose in a round face came bowling up in a white helmet and a blue serge uniform that didn't fit.

'Good morning, Mr Spolding!' said Mrs Green, delighted to have been rescued. 'My, don't you look smart?'

'Yes,' said Mr Spolding, puffing up his chest until he really was as round as a human could be without being a grapefruit.

'As you can see I have received my official uniform and am now a fully fledgling professional – and look here – my official pamphlet –' Mr Spolding held out a little buff pamphlet. He pronounced it 'pamph*lette*', but Mrs Green didn't have the heart to correct him and Phil was too preoccupied to notice.

'That's lovely, Mr Spolding. Now I really do have to get to work –'

But Mr Spolding wasn't having that.

'No, now, no, no, Mrs Green, you really should listen to this short official warning now that I am a short official – I mean, an offishial,' he said and, planting himself firmly in front of them both, he read from the pamphlet.

'This here pamphlette authorryises me to

round up suspishious persons and put them in a offishy custardy – I mean a fishy custard –'

'I think that's official custody, Mr Spolding,' said Mrs Green, ducking around him. 'Why don't you tell Phil all about it – I've got to get into the shop!'

And she was gone, leaving Phil with Mr Spolding, who had caught hold of his arm, determined at all costs to keep at least one member of his audience captive.

The bell dinged as Mrs Green entered and sniffed the air. Docherty's Household Supplies had the best smell of any place ever. It was a mixture of furniture polish, liquorice, tar and apples. All seemed quiet as Mrs Green called out, 'It's only me, Mrs Docherty!' and pulled on her apron. The shop was very still and silent. Mrs Green was just beginning to think that Mrs Docherty was still in bed (her bedroom was above the shop so she got to smell the lovely smell all day and all night) when all of a sudden a spooky white thing popped up from behind the counter.

Mrs Green gave a little shriek. She didn't believe in ghosts, but when one appeared right there in front of her, she couldn't help getting a fright.

'What on earth's the matter?' said Mrs Docherty.

Mrs Green heaved a sigh of relief, which was closely followed by a yelp of alarm.

'What *have* you done, Mrs Docherty?' she said. 'You're all white.'

'I've just been putting the flour away,' said Mrs Docherty, clapping her hands and sending up a huge cloud of white dust.

Mrs Green groaned. That meant the monthly delivery had been made and that Mrs Docherty had started to unpack it by herself. No matter how many times Mrs Green begged her to wait, Mrs Docherty liked to get on and do it alone because it made her feel responsible and happy. The results, though, were often disastrous. Mrs Green zipped around behind the counter and found Mrs Docherty standing waist deep in a conical mound of flour. Swearing very quietly under her breath, Mrs Green got out the dustpan and brush.

Back at the farm, everything had gone from bad to worse ...

Cyril had done something truly dreadful. He'd opened the pot of special jam the children had made for their father's return. Seeing what he'd done, the Greens had rushed at him and he'd slid the pot down the kitchen table to

Celia. She was trying to pretend she wasn't there and the jar had flown off and smashed to pieces on

the stone flags of the kitchen floor. Then the fighting had started in earnest. They'd chased each other round the farm, pelting each other with hay and rotten apples and bits of cow poo. All Celia's clothes, which had been new and therefore in cardboard boxes and not suitcases, were trampled in the mud and the cousins all absolutely hated one another with a passion. Having exhausted all the possibilities for warfare outside, they were now INSIDE the house, wrestling and scratching and yelling like banshees as they got nearer and nearer the best parlour . . .

The Diary

I have absolutely no idea what day it is because the weather has been so awful I have had to stop writing a diary. It kept getting rained on. We're a bit behind now, which isn't comfy for anyone. People start to worry about what's known as 'going over'. That means having to shoot for longer than was originally budgeted for, and you know what THAT means. It means the film will cost a little bit more. I say 'a little bit'. But films cost so

much per week (I'm not even going to tell you because you would be shocked and possibly not even believe me) that any time you think it might take longer, every single person on the set starts to go a bit green. And all the people who are responsible for paying for the film come down on set and stare at us grimly. It's all very difficult. And no matter how many times you wail, 'But it's not our fault! It's the weather!' it still *is* our fault and we have to do something about it quickly. So it all gets a bit tense and the set nurse (who is called Rachel and has the dirtiest laugh of any medically trained person ever) has to give out a lot more aspirin than usual.

Bill Bailey has been on set for the last three days. It's awfully difficult not to throw myself at his feet in a spontaneous act of worship every time he passes. He's playing Farmer Macreadie in a wonderfully battered old felt hat. Darling Danny Mays (Blenkinsop) is back and

My great-grandad was in 'Ben Hur', you know.

we are hoping to finish Scene 54, where the children come back with the piglets, but it is horribly complicated. Nine – count them – NINE actors (all of whom have to get a close-up), seven LIVE SQUEALING piglets, a large horse, a cart, and depressed chickens in the rain. It's hellish. Quite an emotional scene too, so there's a lot of acting required. Yikes.

2 p.m.-ish: You see, it's hot now. And the good thing about the rain was that I didn't get hot. It's very hot indeed in the full Nanny McPhee costume, I can tell

you. A big fat-suit over my own fat, then several layers of heavy black material, pretend boobs (very heavy – they are made of silicone and are what people use to replace a boob if they have lost one in an operation. Sometimes I whip one out unexpectedly – grown men have been known to faint . . .) a hump and a front hump, pretend ears, nose, warts and a wig. It's no fun in there. In the sun, I just gently trickle with sweat all day long. It crawls down my shoulder blades like a tickly worm and I can't reach to scratch. Also, my teeth are hurting. I have a big set up at the top and plumpers in

my cheeks that attach to my lower teeth. They are brilliantly made, but after a few hours, anything pushed in your mouth like that would begin to ache. Nobody's fault. My make-up was designed by Peter King (he won an Oscar for doing all the Lord of the Rings make-up) – who is immensely clever and very good fun. It is all applied by my Welsh make-up artist, Paula Price, who is nothing short of angelic. When I need to be in my full Nanny make-up, she has to get up at 4.30 a.m., drive from Cardiff, meet me at 6 a.m.-ish and start by sticking on my nose with very strong glue. Then my ears, my warts, my monobrow and my wig. And she's called an artist because she *paints* them into my face so that you can't see the join. And you really can't – it looks absolutely real even if you are close to me and peering like anything. It is important to like your artist because they get very near to your face very early in the day. I

Oink! Oink! Oink!

am lucky because I don't just *like* Paula, I *love* her. I do, however, make much less of a fuss than the piglets. They are having their black spots painted on at the moment. This involves being lovingly cradled by Guillaume and gently painted by Gary. They kick up the most unbelievable racket, like a gigantic bucket of angry babies. It's really quite upsetting for everyone. Silly creatures. They don't know how lucky they are.

The Story

Let's leave the children to it for a moment and get back to Phil. We left him outside the shop, still desperate to get Mrs Green to sign and very, very worried about what might happen to him if she wouldn't.

As he walked through the lovely little village he felt slightly comforted by the distance he had put between himself and the threat. After all, nothing truly nasty could ever happen in such a pretty place, could it? Just as he was having this thought, he passed an ivy-clad alley and heard a curious noise, a bit like a cuckoo calling, only more flirtatious.

'Oo-oo!' it went. 'Oo-oo!'

Phil realised that it was a woman's voice – a young woman at that, and sounding so friendly and charming and cheeky and fun. He gave his hair a quick smooth down and looked up the alley. Almost at once he was lifted off his feet by something very strong and deposited against the wall of the alley in a breathless heap. The very strong something turned out to be a gigantic lady in a crimplene suit and high heels. She was very blonde. Next to her was a much smaller but equally blonde person in a sharp little suit and hat. They both smiled sweetly at Phil.

'Hello, Mr Green,' said the little one. Her voice was so attractive. It had a constant bubbling laugh in it as though she found everyone and everything delightful and amazing.

'We haven't met, but I'm Miss Topsey and this is my colleague, Miss Turvey.'

Now of course we know a little about Miss Topsey and Miss Turvey (none of it good), but don't forget that Phil didn't. He'd never seen them before in his life. So when Miss Topsey said, in that lovely way of hers, 'Can you guess who sent us?' for a split second Phil actually thought that word of his utter gorgeousness had spread to the neighbouring villages and this lady had come to check him out.

'Sent two lovelies like yourselves?' he said, winking meaningfully at Miss Topsey so that she knew he meant just her and not the frighteningly strong one. 'Father Christmas?'

Miss Topsey laughed in a trilling soprano for a very long time – longer, Phil thought, than was absolutely necessary, given that he already knew she thought he was irresistible.

'Oh no, Phil! Guess again!'

Before Phil had time to ask himself how she knew his first name, the big scary one spoke.

'Mrs Biggles.'

Phil panicked. He tried to scrabble up the wall but Miss Turvey pulled him back down, he tried to get past her but she was immovable, and when he tried to get past Miss Topsey she tripped him up and both of them leaned over him, so close that he could see the cracks in their lipstick.

'We need the farm, Phil,' said Miss Topsey, her little teeth glinting like pearls in her mouth.

'And we need it now,' breathed Miss Turvey.

Phil started to pant. 'Thing is,' he said. 'Thing is, is it's not exactly all mine, see. It belongs half to me and half to my brother –'

'Half a farm's no good to us, Phil,' said Miss Topsey, more sweetly than ever. 'And the fact is, Mrs Big's told us to come back with one of two things, Phil: the deeds to your farm –'

'Or your kidneys,' said Miss Turvey succinctly.

'Think about it!' they both chimed, making way for Phil to back off down the alley in a state of sheer terror.

The Diary

Beautiful weather. It's 1st June, so that bodes well. We're doing a bunch of pick-ups, just to mop up all the stuff we didn't get earlier this week. We're doing Celia being spattered by the mud. This involves a wonderful contraption composed of a big tyre inside a metal sheath, which is switched on so that the tyre whirls around in the air and is then lowered on to a big pile of mud so it spatters whoever's in front of it. There's a large man in a white cover-all and sunglasses standing in for Rosie Taylor-Ritson, the girl who plays Celia.

Rosie is a miraculous girl who seems to have come from another world where girls are made of bone china, strawberries and cream. Within, she is very strong and capable of doing whatever you might ask her to do. In this case, stand still with her eyes open in front of a gigantic tyre which is about to splatter her with pretend mud. We are all full of admiration.

Nice and relaxed feel today. Miracle, really.

The Story

Back at the shop, Mrs Green was just getting her coat on to leave when she heard noises behind the counter.

'What're you doing back there, Mrs Docherty?' she enquired nervously.

'Oh, nothing at all, dear. Just putting away the treacle.'

Mrs Green gasped and flew round the counter to find all the drawers oozing stickily.

'Goodnight, dear! See you tomorrow! *What* a good day it's been!' sang Mrs Docherty as she floated into the back of the shop and out of sight.

Mrs Green, feeling utterly defeated, slumped against a barrel of oats.

'What am I to do? What am I to do about the farm? What am I to do about the children fighting all the time? What am I to do about the harvest? What if Rory –' but she couldn't finish that thought and quickly moved to an easier one. 'And what am I to do with SEVENTEEN DRAWERS FULL OF TREACLE!!!??'

Then something very strange happened. One of the treacly drawers opened all by itself. From within it issued a deep, syrupy voice which said:

'The person you need is Nanny McPhee.'

Mrs Green got such a shock that she dropped her coat in the puddle of treacle. 'What?' she whispered.

Another drawer, a littler one this time, now opened and a smaller voice came out of it. 'The person you need,' it said, sounding slightly irritated that she hadn't heard it the first time, 'is Nanny McPhee.'

'Who?' said Mrs Green, in a very high voice owing to fright and general surprise about the fact that she was having a conversation with the furniture. Then all the smallest drawers started to open and shut, all squeaking, 'The person you need – the person you need – the person you need –'

Mrs Green picked up her sticky coat and ran.

As she flew out of the door, Mrs Docherty appeared. She looked at the drawers approvingly. They'd all fallen silent.

'– is Nanny McPhee,' said Mrs Docherty, quietly closing the drawers.

Mrs Green legged it home as fast as she could. There was a high wind blowing and as she came into the yard she heard a loud squawk. Looking up, she came face-to-face with a raggedy jackdaw. It was staring at her as though they had, at some point, been formally introduced and she ought to recognise it. Spooked and puzzled and buffeted, she turned away and saw something unfamiliar trodden into the mud. It looked furry. She bent down and saw two beady little eyes peeping up at her. Giving a slight shriek, she was about to run into the house when she realised that the eyes were, in fact, beads and that they belonged to a fox-fur tippet which she now gingerly pulled out of its squelchy ditch.

What in heaven's name was a fox-fur tippet doing in the farmyard?

Mrs Green gave a sudden gasp of realisation and horror. There was only one person she knew who could afford such an expensive item and that was Prunella. But it was such a teeny-weeny tippet that it must be a child's. It followed, therefore, that Prunella's child Celia must be nearby. And it also followed therefore that she and her brother had arrived early and must have been attacked in some way.

And lastly, it followed that the noises she now heard issuing from the farmhouse, loud enough to be heard above the howling wind and squawking jackdaw, were the noises of battle.

'Oh no!' gulped Mrs Green. 'Oh no, no, no, no, no, no, no.'

She went to the door. Huge thuds and screams came from behind it. She opened it, her heart in her mouth.

The sight that met her eyes was little less than catastrophic.

Norman had Cyril in a headlock and was dragging him around in circles, letting out the most dreadful war cries. Cyril was kicking at

Norman, while above them, on the landing, Megsie was pulling pieces off Celia's dress and trying to tie her to the banisters with them as Celia made violent attempts to escape, shrieking, 'Let go, let *go*, let GO.'

'All right then,' said Megsie, letting go and causing Celia to catapult down the stairs as Vincent appeared with his father's cricket bat, thumping everything he could see and yelling, 'Death, death, death and hurting!' over and over again.

Taking a deep breath, Mrs Green walked in and was immediately spun around by the battling boys.

'Celia! Cyril! You're early!' she screamed. 'How's your mother?'

The children took not the blindest bit of notice and continued to wrestle and screech until Mrs Green had to stop her ears and thunder, 'STOP! STOP FIGHTING!!!'

But no one could hear her. Just at that moment there was a thundering rap at the door. Lightning illuminated the room and Mrs Green whirled to see a very odd, lumpy silhouette through the glass bit of the door.

'What on earth . . .' she breathed, when there it was again. RAT-A-TAT-TAT. A heavy, no nonsense, answer-this-door-immediately kind of knocking.

Mrs Green went to the door feeling a

trepidation quite unlike anything she had ever experienced before. She took hold of the door knob and threw open the door. As she did so, lightning blazed across the sky, allowing her to see in intense detail the person who was standing in the porch.

It was female, of that there could be no doubt. A vast and hideous female, dressed from head to foot in rusty black stuff trimmed with jet. But the face! Her face was so UGLY, so ugly you could hardly believe it. Her nose was like a giant pocky old potato. Her eyebrows met bushily in the middle and she had two enormous black hairy warts like spiders! Out over her lip stuck a gigantic and discoloured tombstone-shaped tooth and she stared at Mrs Green out of ancient glittering eyes.

Mrs Green was entirely unable to speak. Even though she had been taught from a very early age that it was rude to stare, she simply couldn't help it. She stared and stared and then she stared some more.

The fierce-looking female stared back for a short moment. Then she opened her mouth to speak. It seemed strange that anyone with quite so many enormous teeth should be able to speak at all, but when she did, it was in a calm, almost mellifluous way.

'Good evening, Mrs Green. I am Nanny McPhee.'

Mrs Green realised she had stopped breathing, took in a big lungful of air and tried to address her visitor as politely as she knew she ought.

'Oh, *you're it*! I mean him – her – the Nanny they – I do beg your pardon – who?'

Unperturbed, and casting a glance at the violence that continued without interruption behind Mrs Green, the strange person spoke again.

'Nanny McPhee. Small *c*. Big *p*.'

Mrs Green felt that the last thing she needed was someone this scary-looking trying to interfere.

'Yes, I see, righto, but the thing is – the thing is that I haven't hired a nanny – you see? I don't – I've never – I don't actually like nannies and I'm managing perfectly well here –'

This was the moment Norman chose to pick Vincent up and throw him bodily at Cyril. Nanny McPhee raised her single bushy eyebrow at poor Mrs Green.

'It's the war!' said Mrs Green, somewhat hysterically. 'It's not a very good influence.'

All the children were now in the best parlour,

bashing each other and screaming louder than ever. Mrs Green backed away from the front door and closed the door to the parlour. When she turned around, Nanny McPhee was in the house with the front door closed and even though Mrs Green knew she hadn't *exactly* invited her in, something very deep inside her seemed to be saying, 'Yes, do come in, please do come in.'

'Tea?' said Mrs Green, trying to lead Nanny McPhee away from the parlour into the kitchen.

'Perhaps later,' said Nanny McPhee calmly. 'Let me just introduce myself to the children.'

Mrs Green panicked. 'Oh no! No, no – I mean – wait – I mean – have you got any references?'

Nanny McPhee turned and fixed Mrs Green with a penetrating stare.

'I am an army nanny, Mrs Green. I have been deployed. Why don't you put the kettle on?'

And again, while every conscious thought inside Mrs Green's head was screaming, 'Get out of my house you scary thing' another voice, deep inside her, was saying gently, 'Yes, let's put the kettle on. What a good idea.'

So she turned to put the kettle on, and when she turned back the kitchen was empty.

The Diary

Back in the studio now. Hot in there, but I'm surviving. We took three days to shoot the Greens fighting over the lemon drop and now we're starting on another three-day marathon. Maggie Gyllenhaal, our beautiful, harassed Mrs Green, had to shout so much during the lemon drop bit that she lost her voice! She was heroic. The children coped gamely with the heat and all the smoke they pump into the set to make it look more real. (I know that sounds peculiar but it's true – the smoke softens everything somehow and makes it look lived in. They call it 'atmos', which is short for 'atmosphere'.)

Simon's set is genuinely breathtaking.

Maggie G., by the way, has come all the way from America with her husband and her little girl (who is only four) to live on our rainy island for THREE MONTHS. We are all very proud she is here with us, and when Susanna, Lindsay and I sit at the monitor to watch her, we sometimes gasp and hold on to each other because she is so, so beautiful.

We've had some seriously bad news – Rhys Ifans, our Phil, has broken his foot showing some six-year-olds a few nifty football moves. It's always something tiny that causes an accident, but the implications for the shoot are enormous. David Brown's rushing around trying to sort it out. We can't shoot on him until August and it's only June! Yikes.

Shepperton Studios is its usual collection of huts, stages and car parks but very pleasant even so. And no problems with the weather, of course, because we're shooting indoors. I am in the full Nanny gear, with the cape and everything. So far it hasn't been too hot.

Later: I spoke too soon. Nose has peeled off and refuses to be re-stuck. Paula will have to put on a new one. Did

I tell you she keeps them in the fridge? Because she does.

I can't eat or laugh in this get-up. Talking's hard too. Let's face it, this costume does inhibit most of life's major pleasures. It is, however, one of the most effective costumes I've ever worn, so hats off to the Costume Department (see Glossary).

The Story

In the best parlour, the violence was escalating. Vincent was still bashing at the furniture with his cricket bat but being careful not to dent anything too precious. Megsie now had Celia in a fireman's lift and was smacking her bottom with the fire-tongs while Norman and Cyril were busy pushing each other's heads into the wall.

The door opened and in glided Nanny McPhee. No one took much notice. Norman flung her a glance and managed to grunt out a 'Who are YOU?' before being slammed on to the sofa.

'I am Nanny McPhee,' replied the ghastly-looking stranger. 'Please listen carefully. You are all to stop what you are doing and go upstairs to bed.'

Now, it was an odd thing, because although Nanny McPhee spoke far too softly to be heard above the din, nonetheless every word dropped into each child's ear as clear as a silver bell.

But did they do what they were told?

Of course they didn't! They were far too busy fighting and screaming.

'Did you hear what I said?'

Again, they heard it, every single word. But Norman just yelled, 'Ha! A nanny for the namby-pamby townies!' before proceeding to kick Cyril hard in the shins.

Nanny McPhee gazed at them all and narrowed her eyes. Her long black cloak moved and from underneath it she produced a strange, knobbly stick.

Raising it, she brought it down to the floor with a sharp bang that seemed to echo through the house. The children were far too busy to notice the golden sparks that spattered from the bottom of the stick and escaped under the door. But they did all stop, just for a second, to stare at her.

'Was that supposed to impress us?' Cyril sneered. Nanny McPhee looked at him expressionlessly. He shrugged his shoulders and raised a fist to thump Norman.

And then the oddest thing occurred. Instead of thumping Norman, his fist, as though in the grip of an invisible puppeteer, twisted at the end of his arm and tried to thump *him*, missing twice before grabbing his own collar and throwing him to the floor.

Cyril, winded by the fall and the surprise, just lay there panting, with his eyes as round as golf balls. Norman sniggered and pointed. Cyril's hand then yanked Cyril about and thwacked him hard on the head. Now Norman laughed out loud as everyone else stared in astonishment.

'What on *earth* are you doing, Cyril?' said Celia, as, very suddenly, Norman clutched his own ear and pulled himself across the room squealing with pain.

Even if Cyril had been in any position to answer her, Celia would not have noticed. She was too busy grabbing her own hair and pulling it very hard. Her eyes were screwed up so tight against the stinging that she didn't even notice Megsie hitting her own bottom hard with the fire-tongs and yelping, 'It's happening to me too!'

Meanwhile, Vincent, his eyes like saucers, suddenly felt the cricket bat twitch in his hand. He stared at it apprehensively. Very suddenly it

jerked itself up into the air and came down very hard on the best mahogany table, giving it a terrific dent.

'Oh no!!' cried Vincent, trying to drop the bat. But it seemed stuck fast to his hands and now he started to go about the room whacking and whacking and whacking whatever got in the way. Ornaments went flying, crockery smashed and Vincent, terrified, started to yell, 'Stop, stop, stop, stop!!!' at the top of his voice.

Hearing Vincent, the other children yelled as well. 'Stop!' Norman shrieked as he shoved his own head into the horn of the gramophone player, and 'Stop!' shouted Celia as she yanked out handfuls of her own hair, and 'Stop!' screamed Cyril as he rhythmically head-banged a footstool and 'Please stop!' howled Megsie as she smacked her cheeks in turn until they were bright pink.

Oh, it was awful. And during all this, Nanny McPhee stood quietly, calmly, just watching. I don't know which one it was who worked out that she must have caused this peculiar and

painful behaviour, but suddenly all the children were looking at her and begging her to stop them.

'Please stop us!!' they cried.

'On one condition,' said Nanny McPhee. 'That you apologise for hurting each other and promise to stop fighting.'

Almost immediately, Norman yelled, 'Never!'

Nanny McPhee raised her monobrow.

'Never!' shouted Cyril. 'They started it!'

'Never!' cried Megsie, but not with much conviction. Celia didn't shout at all – she was staring in horror at the pile of hair growing at her feet.

'Granny's little shepherdess!' shouted Vincent, heartbroken as all his family's beloved knick-knacks were smashed by the merciless cricket bat. Behind him lay a trail of china – Mrs Green's best tea service was completely destroyed and Vincent was almost in tears. But something much worse was about to occur. The bat was pulling him towards the fireplace and the mantelpiece.

WHACK! it went and the first part of the mantelpiece started to crack. There, at the other end, was the little blue bundle of Dad's precious letters, tied with a ribbon.

'No! NO, no, no!!! Dad's letters! They're going to get burnt!'

Norman and Megsie looked. Sure enough, the letters were beginning to slide down the broken mantelpiece and would be in the flames in seconds.

Megsie panicked. 'All right!! I apologise! I'm sorry I hurt you, Celia! I promise to stop fighting!'

Norman's pride was very strong, but the letters from his father were too important. They were all they had and if his father were never to return – but that was too painful a thought, more painful even than the thought of apologising to the invaders. 'I'm sorry too! I'm sorry, Cyril – I promise to stop fighting!' he blurted out. Then all the children started shouting at once, begging and begging Nanny McPhee to stop them. Only Cyril stubbornly refused to speak.

Nanny McPhee said, very quietly, 'All of you.'

Now everyone turned towards Cyril and

started shrieking at him. The loudest of all was Celia.

'Cyril, apologise NOW OR I'LL END UP BALD!!'

Cyril wound his tie around his own neck and started to yank it backwards and forwards. He was tired and in pain and he was fond of his sister and genuinely concerned about the bald patches appearing on her skull. He started to apologise but it was too late. 'NOOOOO!!' cried all the Green children, twisting around to watch the precious letters as they plummeted towards the flames.

BANG!

The stick came down again. Everything froze except for Nanny McPhee. She was about to cross the room to gather up the letters, which were suspended above the frozen flames, when something suddenly swooped into the room from an open window and snatched the letters up in its beak, delivering them to Nanny McPhee before standing at her feet looking up at her with an expression of intense longing. It was the raggedy jackdaw. Nanny McPhee eyed him beadily.

'What on earth are you doing in here, Mr Edelweiss? I thought I told you to stop following me.'

The jackdaw squawked. Nanny McPhee tutted irritably.

'No, you most certainly are not forgiven. You know what you did. Now make yourself scarce.'

Uttering a mournful squawk, the jackdaw flew out of the window. Nanny McPhee banged her stick, this time very gently. The frozen children started to move again. They stared at their hands, at each other, at the room, which had been entirely restored to perfect condition and, finally, at Nanny McPhee. No one noticed that one of her big, spidery warts had disappeared.

'It is rude to stare,' she said. 'Upstairs to bed, please.'

Too shocked and too relieved to speak, the children all filed out past her into the kitchen. Pausing only to replace the letters on the mantelpiece, Nanny McPhee followed them.

The Diary

Been on set for three hours in the full Nanny costume including the cape. Everything hurts. Teeth, jaw, shoulders, back. Standing becomes tricky because my chest and ribs get pressured by the weight of it all and I can't breathe very well. It's a Wednesday.

Later. Utterly miserable. I am NEVER doing this again.

Later: Greg has come to calm me down. I was about to burst into tears – which would have been DISASTROUS and VERY EXPENSIVE because we'd have had to STOP and REDO the make-up, when he appeared in the doorway and made me laugh instead. Susanna is very grateful and so am I. The most grateful person is Paula, who is going to buy him a beer later. Even so, my nose DID melt and had to be replaced. Had to keep taking everything off to breathe for a bit and put it all back on. Still, at least I'm not playing a Klingon. It's very, very hot and the children have been majestic.

The Story

Chapter Thirty-Seven. (Oh all right, it can't be, but I don't know how to do chapters. This is my first book. Why does one have to chop up a story into chunks? Is it just to give you an excuse to put the book down? That doesn't seem right. It's a new bit anyway – you decide if you want it to be a new chapter.)

Back in the kitchen, time was playing odd tricks, for as soon as Mrs Green had got the teapot down from the dresser, the children came quietly out of the sitting room and past her up the stairs. Nanny McPhee had only just gone in, Mrs Green thought, and so she almost dropped the teapot. When she saw the state of the children, she had to sit down. It was impossible! They were all clean and tidy! They were saying goodnight to her, very politely, and, most miraculous of all, they had stopped fighting!! Nanny McPhee came out too and stood staring at her with an odd little smile at the corner of her mouth.

'These children need five lessons, Mrs Green. Lesson One – to stop fighting – is complete.'

Mrs Green gulped.

'Early beds tonight, I think. Leave it to me. You should have a little time to yourself,' said Nanny McPhee, noiselessly following the last child up to the bedroom.

Mrs Green gulped again. Time to herself? She couldn't remember when anything like that had last happened. She sat for one more astonished moment before leaping to her feet and rushing headlong into the bathroom.

In the bedroom, the children were grouped in two corners of the room, regarding each other in hostile silence. No one quite understood exactly what had happened or *how* it had happened, and no one would dare to fight again, but they were still mortal enemies. Nanny McPhee glided into the room and eyed them all beadily. Then she cleared her throat. Everyone looked at her. The stick was nowhere to be seen.

'I am going to explain to you the way I work,' she said.

'That'll take some doing,' muttered Cyril.

'Do try and remember this,' she continued, ignoring Cyril. 'When you need me but do not want me, then I must stay. When you want me but no longer need me, then I have to go.'

The children frowned. Then Cyril, who was good at being rude when the occasion demanded it, said what they were all thinking.

'How could anyone possibly ever want *you*?'

Instead of being cross, Nanny McPhee gazed at him equably. 'Well, it's an odd thought, I grant you, but there it is,' she said. 'Now, to business. In the absence of any spare beds, Norman, I presume, will be sharing with Cyril?'

'I'd rather share with a goat,' said Norman immediately.

'A goat wouldn't have you,' retorted Cyril.

'I see,' said Nanny McPhee calmly. 'Megsie, Celia – would you be willing to share?'

'I'd rather share with Geraldine,' snapped Megsie.

'She's our cow,' explained Vincent helpfully, busy wondering what he'd rather share his bed with.

'I'm not sharing anything with that vicious harpy!' said Celia.

'And I'd rather share with an elephant!' crowed Vincent, happy to have made a decision. Next to pigs, elephants were his favourite.

'Thank you, Vincent, but you will not be required to share, owing to the size of your bed. The rest of you, however, will have to come to some arrangement.'

'Never!' said Norman,

'Never!' said Megsie,

'Never!' said Celia,

'Never!' said Cyril,

and

'NEVER!' yelled Vincent, delighted to have

the last word for once.

Nanny McPhee frowned. The cloak began to move aside. Uh-oh.

Downstairs, time had been playing funny tricks again, for Mrs Green had had half an hour to have a proper bath and wash her hair. She hadn't been able to have more than a two-minute wash for what felt like months and she felt like a new woman. She looked up the stairs anxiously. All was silent. Except – wait, no, she'd heard a sort of a thud. Well, more like the echo of a thud, more like a little tremor through the house. Then she saw two little golden sparks pattering down the stairs. She rubbed her eyes. When she opened them, the sparks were gone. How odd, she thought. That bath's relaxed me so much I'm seeing things. Perhaps this new nanny was just what they all needed. She was a bit – well – ugly, to be sure, but her results were nothing short of –

'Ahem.'

Mrs Green jumped and found Nanny McPhee in front of her holding a lantern.

'Lesson Two – to share nicely – is complete,' she said.

'What? I mean, how? I mean — that's a miracle — how on earth — how *did* you do it, Nanny McPhee?' said Mrs Green.

'I'm afraid that's classified information, Mrs Green,' said Nanny McPhee, walking towards the kitchen door. 'The army is very strict about such matters.'

'Oh yes, yes, of course,' said Mrs Green, feeling slightly ashamed to have asked at all. 'The thing is,' she went on, very fast so that Nanny McPhee wouldn't leave, 'we can't afford to pay you and we haven't any spare beds but —'

'Please do not trouble yourself, Mrs Green,' said Nanny McPhee. 'The army remunerates me and I have arranged my own accommodation. Goodnight, Mrs Green. Pleasant dreams.'

And with that, the kitchen door quietly opened and Nanny McPhee slid silently out. Mrs Green put her fist into her mouth and bit it. No, she was awake. She hadn't just had an amazing dream about an ugly, free nanny or the fact that she'd had time to wash her ears in the bath. Sighing with contentment, she lifted her tea and took a lovely, long gulp.

Back in the bedroom — and this will come as

no surprise – the children were in bed with their teeth brushed. Megsie and Celia were head-to-toe, as were Norman and Cyril. They were all absolutely furious and determined not to sleep a wink until such time as they could either escape or complain to their mother about the Big Warty Person who was making them do things they didn't want to do. They stared at each other hatefully. Vincent was also being unpleasant, jumping up and down upon his truckle-bed singing, 'I don't have to sha-are, I don't have to sha-are!'

Then something very odd happened. The bedroom door opened and the Green family's cow, Geraldine, walked calmly in and climbed into bed with Megsie and Celia.

The children were so astonished they couldn't speak, but then Megsie got a hoof in her ear and she slapped Geraldine crossly. Geraldine mooed at her just as crossly and flicked her tail into Celia's face.

'Ugh! Get OUT!' said Celia, but something deep within her was already saying, 'This cow's going nowhere. You might as well try to get some sleep.'

As the girls tried to arrange themselves around Geraldine's large and ungainly frame, in walked the goat, Alphonse. He was called Alphonse because it sounded French and the Greens knew that the French had invented perfume and Alphonse had a very strong smell. He, of course, got into bed with Norman and Cyril. The stench was indescribable. The boys kicked and squirmed and tried to push Alphonse out and tried to get out of the bed themselves, but it was no use. They were all stuck with each

other. Vincent, who had been watching it all with a mixture of delight and terror, quickly decided to get in and switch off his light. But there, on his pillow, lay a little trunk, which was attached to a very large lump underneath his quilted blanket. Vincent was left with about three centimetres of bed to sleep in. He curled himself around the little elephant, who was quite warm and already whiffling gently, and fell instantly into a deep sleep.

The house started to fall silent. Even the warring children, anger in their hearts, bruises on their legs and twisted into impossible shapes around their peculiar bedfellows, slept now.

Outside there were more distinctly odd things going on. Near the pigsty, something was moving. But you'll find out about that in the morning.

The Diary

Not in costume today! Hooray! Just in the perfect hell of trying to shoot the jam-smashing sequence in one day, which we have all rightly come to the conclusion is impossible. Susanna's hair is almost standing up on end. Luckily, Irene is there to calm her down. Irene Chawko is our Continuity Lady, or Script Supervisor (see Glossary). She is also an athlete – she does cross-country skiing and is remarkably fit. No matter how hot or how cold it is, Irene always wears the same kind of clothes – Susanna and she once worked together in the desert and apparently Irene still wore cotton polo-necks, even though it was 40 degrees in the shade. What we have shot is very good, but we are behind now and that always makes people look depressed and concerned. Any minute now Eric will turn up and glower at us. I don't care. I am not in my costume. I am wearing leggings and a T-shirt. I am completely happy.

Next day: In early – I mean not ordinary early, which is 6.30-ish, but actually early, which is 6 (having got into the car at 5). We are shooting the bit where the animals walk into the kitchen. On another stage, the animal wranglers are working with Beryl (there's no mud so she's happy), and on this set, I am pretending to be Beryl. It would take too long to try to shoot Beryl on the real set because it takes ages to get her up the stairs. It's no problem to get her *in*, the difficulty is getting her *out*. Gary, who is working with her, says she has a great sense of timing. She always looks towards where Mrs Green would be if she were there at exactly the right moment. How amazing. A *humorous* cow.

We have had some really

What do you expect? I'm a professional.

I just don't *do* mud. Get a stand-in for that.

sad news though. One of the main reasons I wrote this script was so that I would have the chance to work with a baby elephant. Everyone was excited, and early this year the search began. We found the most wonderful baby called Riddle at Whipsnade. He was the perfect age and he had already been trained by a fantastic team. He could do all sorts of things and I was waiting with bated breath for the day we could all go off to Whipsnade and shoot his section of the story. Alas, we heard this morning that a virus that attacks only elephants had got to him and killed him. They are all devastated in the office. Can't imagine how the team at Whipsnade are feeling. Baby elephants are quite vulnerable to infection, apparently. David Brown actually met Riddle and is in a state of grief. So now we have no live elephant and will have to have a pretend one that the special effects team will produce. It will be brilliant, of course it will, but it's very upsetting altogether. In fact, I'm so depressed I'm going back to the story.

The Story

Cyril woke the next morning to find no goat in the bed but two feet on the pillow next to him.

'Argh!!! My feet!' he cried, grabbing them. A very cross Norman yanked them away.

'Oh. They're yours,' said Cyril, with relief, and suddenly a very loud tooting on a trumpet woke all the others up too.

Everyone sat up and looked around. All the animals were gone, and everyone was exceptionally glad about that except Vincent, who was already missing his elephant.

'Rise and shine,' said Nanny McPhee briskly. She was in an enormous smart black uniform, also trimmed with jet, with black pointy boots which were rather little when you considered what they had to carry about.

'Beds made – hospital corners, if you please – and downstairs for breakfast at the double!' And with that she turned smartly on her heel and left the room. There was a short, subdued silence.

Then Megsie spoke: 'Who *is* she? And how did she do all those things?'

Cyril puffed out his chest. 'I have a theory,' he said.

'Oh, here we go,' muttered Norman, getting under his pillow. But he listened all the same.

'I think she's a secret weapon. My father's very high up in the War Office and I know about these things. I think that stick of hers releases some sort of gas that makes people and animals do strange things. I'm going to write to Father and report her. He'll have her called off.'

Cyril sounded so sure of himself that for a moment all the Greens thought, Yes, that must be it. She's a secret weapon. Lord Gray will have her called off.

But then Celia piped up. 'Don't be silly, Cyril. Father never even replies to your letters, you know that.'

Cyril coloured. Norman, interested, came out from under his pillow to look at him. Cyril stared angrily back as Vincent said, 'That's like our dad. He hasn't replied to our letters for years and years.'

Now it was Cyril and Celia's turn to look interested.

'That's not true, Vinnie,' said Megsie crossly.

'Three months, that's all, since the last one,' said Norman, not wanting the vile cousins to think that the wonderful Mr Green was anything like their father.

'He's in the army. They move them around a lot. Letters get lost.'

'Does your dad move around a lot then too?' asked Vincent, intrigued.

'No,' said Cyril shortly. 'He's always in the same office.'

There was a silence which no one quite knew how to break. Finally, Celia said, 'Well, I'm jolly well staying in bed till Mummy comes.'

Now Norman hopped out. 'No one stays in bed around here. There's chores to do. Come on, you lot – time to feed the animals!'

'Yes, I expect you're all hungry by now,' said Cyril, who was wearing purple silk pyjamas.

'Oh, ha ha,' said Norman, grabbing his clothes and leaving, followed by a very sulky Megsie and Vincent.

'I suppose we'll have to get up to get fed,' said Cyril, who was used to a valet bringing him breakfast in bed every morning except Sundays, when everyone met for devilled kidneys in a very long and chilly dining room. He put on his monogrammed slippers, grabbed a little case from the bed-knob and headed out. 'You coming?' he asked Celia, none too gently.

'Don't be silly. I haven't a thing to wear,' said Celia crossly. Cyril had heard this many times before and never believed it, but this time it was manifestly true. All Celia's precious new clothes were lying in the mud around the house.

Celia lay in bed in her slip. She was hungry. She had to find something to wear. Those horrible peasanty children had destroyed her clothes. They owed her new things. She decided to get up and explore. There must be something somewhere she could wear until her mother came for her.

Downstairs, Mrs Green was ready for work and had even managed to have a quiet breakfast on her own. Nanny McPhee was there, doling out porridge to a group of sullen faces. Cyril was sitting in the window seat wearing his gas mask. Mrs Green looked at him worriedly.

'Cyril, dear, why are you wearing your gas mask?' she enquired somewhat timidly, because she was feeling guilty about Celia's clothes.

'In case of a GAS ATTACK, Aunt Isabel,' said Cyril, staring very pointedly at Nanny McPhee.

'A gas attack? Cyril, I don't think there's going to be a gas attack here, we're in the middle of nowhere – that's why your mother sent you here, remember?'

Cyril rudely ignored her and took his porridge as far away from the others as he could.

Mrs Green stared at them all and wrung her hands. 'Oh dear, Nanny McPhee. Sharing nicely doesn't seem to have cheered them up much.'

'One step at a time,' said Nanny McPhee.

'Yes. Yes, of course. I must run. There's a delivery of mousetraps at the shop today and I simply must get to them before Mrs Docherty,' and casting one more worried look at the moping children, she pulled on her coat and ran out of the door.

'Right,' said Norman. 'Chores. Megs, you feed Geraldine, Vinnie, you collect the eggs, I'll check the barley, and Cyril, you can sweep up the dung.'

'I'd love to sweep up the dung,' said Cyril silkily, 'but alas, I appear to have left my dung-sweepers at home. Perhaps Celia could be of assistance?'

Norman just scowled. He was about to shoo everyone out to start work when Celia came downstairs wearing something white and pearly-looking. Megsie choked on her porridge.

'What are you wearing?' she said in a shocked whisper as soon as she'd caught her breath.

Celia looked down and fingered the pretty material.

'Um — I think it's mostly tulle,' she said, pleased that Megsie, who wouldn't know an item of haute couture if it bit her on the ankle, was taking an interest.

Megsie got up and pointed an accusing finger at Celia. 'That's our mother's wedding dress!' she said. 'Take it off at once!'

Oh dear. This is what had happened. Unable, of course, to find anything suitable in the children's bedroom, Celia had tiptoed into Mr and Mrs Green's room and rifled through their wardrobe. She'd felt a little guilty but had justified her actions by remembering all her spoilt new things lying in the mud. There hadn't been much in the wardrobe — a few frocks, darned and mended many times over, and a depressing pinafore or two, nothing she could possibly have countenanced wearing. But then she'd found a pretty box in one of the drawers. She'd opened it and found a lovely little floaty dress in pearly white with, of all things, a veil. She'd tried it on and it had fitted quite well and there she was, looking presentable, ready for when her mother arrived to take her home.

'Wedding dress? What — this old thing?' said

Celia disbelievingly. 'No, it can't be. Look – it hasn't even got a train.' And she twirled round so that Megsie could see how wrong she'd been.

Now I *know* that what Celia had done was rather awful and rude, but you must remember she really didn't have anything to wear and she came from a world where wedding dresses were kept either in their own special trunks in rooms set apart from the rest of the house or in the vaults of banks if they were encrusted with particularly precious gems. Her mother's dress had had a train that was twenty feet long and covered in doves' feathers and diamonds, so try to understand – the poor girl had no idea that other people were different. No one had ever thought to tell her. The puffball dress was the sort of thing her mother might have worn to a coffee morning, and not a very posh one at that. But Megsie wasn't to know this and she lunged at Celia violently, yelling, 'Take it OFF!! TAKE IT OFF!!!'

Celia shrieked and ran behind a chair as Nanny McPhee stood, watching the proceedings with her usual calm.

'Help me get it off her!' shouted Megsie but

everyone except Cyril had already gone off to do their chores. Casting a defiant glance at Nanny McPhee, Megsie was just about to pull the dress off Celia by force when Norman rushed back into the kitchen, white to the teeth.

'The piglets have escaped! They've all gone!!'

Vincent, behind him, was practically in tears. Norman was frantic.

'Everyone – now – you've got to help us, quickly, we have to catch them, I need *all* of you – Cyril, Celia, come quickly –'

But Cyril and Celia had no intention of going anywhere. Norman went up to Cyril and faced him square on.

'Listen, Cyril – these are prize piglets. The money we get from them will pay for the tractor hire and that will mean we can get the harvest in – if we don't get the harvest in, we could lose the farm – we promised our dad we'd look after it. *Now* will you help us?'

For answer, Cyril calmly started to file his nails. Norman looked as if he wanted very much to hit Cyril but there was no time and, anyway, Nanny McPhee had made them promise and he had a nasty feeling that breaking that promise would not help him find the piglets. He turned, feeling hopeless, to Megsie and said, 'Come on then. We'll just have to try on our own.' And out he ran, followed by Megsie and Vincent, who paused only to yell resentfully at Cyril, 'You'd help if it was *your* dad's farm, wouldn't you?'

When they'd gone, the room was very quiet. Cyril sensed Nanny McPhee's gaze on him and whirled to face her.

'And you can't make me, either!' he shouted, 'I've got my gas mask, and that stick of yours won't work!'

Almost by way of an answer, Nanny McPhee quietly leant her stick against the table and stepped away from it. Cyril thought he had won, but there was a little voice inside his head that simply would not be quiet. It kept saying: 'If it was *your* dad . . . if it was *your* dad . . . if it was *your* dad . . .' over and over.

Finally, he couldn't stand it any more. He flung away his gas mask, muttered, 'Oh blast you all!' and marched out of the door. Nanny McPhee gave a little smile, picked up her stick and turned to Celia, who had come out from behind the chair to see where Cyril had gone. She saw Nanny McPhee coming towards her and panicked.

'No. Oh no, no, no, no, no. I simply can't run in these heels,' she said, backing up against the staircase and screwing up her eyes in fright. When she opened them again, Nanny McPhee was standing in front of her holding a pair of wellies.

The Diary

Am very glum today. Gaia (my daughter, who's nine) is fed up with me not being at home for four nights a week. I reassured her by reminding her that school hols start next week and she'll be able to come and stay with me and be on set. Her big brother, Tindy, is working as the Video Assist (see Glossary), so she's also a bit jealous of him. Whatever it is, it's never any fun when your children are sad.

In studio it's hotter than the hottest bit of the Sahara on an unusually hot day. There are huge tubes hanging around, pointing into the set and blowing cold air about the place – it looks like we're in the complicated section of a giant's stomach. But there never quite seems to be enough cool air to cool it down, unless, that is, you stand in front of the end of one of the tubes, in which case you look like something the giant's just eaten.

However – and oddly – on the parlour set it is rather COLD because there are no lights in it or pointing at it. I'm hoping that soon, when the very hot air meets the cold air, some kind of weather front will be created and it will start to rain. It wouldn't help filming but it would be very exciting.

The reason it gets so hot in studio is that when we are shooting bits that take place during the day, we have to make it look like it's a sunny day outside and for this we use gigantic great lights about the size of a small car. When these behemoths are switched on they belt out incredible heat. If you stood in front of one for longer than a few seconds you'd probably get burnt. And there are several of them, so that's why the temperature soars and we all get sweaty and grumpy and have to drink eighty-seven gallons of water an hour. It's really quite unpleasant now I come to think about it. The Sparks (see Glossary) are all very apologetic, especially Paul, the Gaffer (see Glossary), who is very polite and says things like, 'Do forgive us, ma'am,' when it's hot.

The Story

All the children were off trying to find the piglets. Nanny McPhee was in the garden sniffing the air when she heard a very familiar noise. It was a sort of squawky burp. She sighed to herself and turned to find the jackdaw, Mr Edelweiss, standing on the garden fence looking sheepish.

'You have the collywobbles again, haven't you?' said Nanny McPhee sternly. Mr Edelweiss tried to deny it but another burp popped out and he flew around in a small, distressed circle before landing on the fence again, this time a little farther away.

'You've been eating window putty again, haven't you?' she said, even more sternly.

Mr Edelweiss jumped up and down, flew off to do a burp behind the barn, flew back and squawked again, this time with some urgency.

'I'm not interested in anything you might have to tell me, Mr Edelweiss. You are a destructive person with revolting habits. Our relationship is over,' said Nanny McPhee, turning her back on him. Very upset, Mr

Edelweiss flew around her head squawking loudly and persistently. All of a sudden Nanny McPhee went very still.

'Really?' she said. 'That *is* interesting. Show me.'

Delighted, Mr Edelweiss led Nanny McPhee around the barn to where a small stream ran and the peelings were composted. There was a strong smell of rotting vegetation. There, at the foot of the barn wall, was a hole, a very large hole that led to a tunnel that had clearly been dug by something or someone very big.

'Hmph,' said Nanny McPhee. 'How very odd. That's far too big for the piglets to have dug, and it must be how they escaped. Hmph.'

She and Mr Edelweiss went into the barn and found the entrance to the tunnel behind the feeding trough. This made Nanny McPhee very thoughtful and cured Mr Edelweiss's colly-wobbles. They both made their way out into the sunshine and Mr Edelweiss flew to the top of the dovecote to see if there was any sign of the children or the piglets. In the distance, he could see Vincent and Megsie and Celia. They were all carrying piglets. He reported his sightings to Nanny McPhee, who, instead of looking pleased, frowned and lifted her stick. Mr Edelweiss squawked in fright.

'Well, we don't want to make it too easy for them,' she said, and down came the stick, scattering golden sparkles all through the yard, which the chickens tried, unsuccessfully, to eat.

Out in the fields, this is what had been happening. Cursing his pricking conscience, Cyril had run after Norman doggedly for some time and was just catching up with him as Norman spotted a piglet under a tree, rootling.

Norman, amazed to see Cyril at all, shushed him and indicated the piglet. Silently, they both started to move in on it.

Over in the next-door field, Celia, now in wellies, had run up to Vincent and Megsie saying, 'I'm only helping till Mummy comes,' and now was cooing with delight over the piglet in Vincent's arms, which was so pretty and pink and sweet. I'm not sure the children felt it, but that was the moment when a strange tremor ran through the land, as though there might just have been a very minor earthquake. Megsie was about to give Celia her piglet so she could look out for another one when both hers and Vincent's made a sudden wriggle and leapt out of their arms, racing like mad things towards the pond.

Megsie screeched.

'This is all your fault!' she shouted at Celia, which wasn't very fair, but then she had to race down the hill to catch up with the piglets. Celia and Vincent followed.

Meanwhile, Norman and Cyril had closed right in on their piglet. Norman made a sign and they both grabbed for it at once. But the piglet slipped through their hands, jumped on to the trunk of the tree, RAN UP IT, and then wandered along a branch looking down at the boys and sniggering. Norman and Cyril stood there with their mouths hanging open.

'Is that normal?' said Cyril, after a long moment.

'No. No, it's not,' said Norman.

'I see. Well, how are we going to get it down?'

As though it had heard, the piglet ran down to the end of the branch and *somersaulted* off it into the undergrowth, turning for a second to make sure the children had seen it and then running away.

'Do they all have circus skills?' asked Cyril, who, having never been to the country, had no idea just how peculiar a pig doing a somersault was. But Norman was already chasing after the piglet.

Cyril followed, his fatigue forgotten in the thrill of the chase and the hugely entertaining nature of the piglets.

Back at the pond, it looked as though the children were going to catch their piglets again without any problem – the pond was in front of them and there was no escape either side. Pigs aren't very good swimmers, so Megsie slowed down and gestured to Celia and Vincent to do the same. They crept up on the piglets, who were looking around as if they realised they were trapped. But then another very odd thing occurred. The piglets looked at the children, chortled and suddenly DIVED balletically into the pond, making a sort of *whee!* noise.

Megsie gasped, Celia pointed and Vincent gave a shout of surprise.

'We'll have to go in after them,' said Megsie, starting to take off her wellies. But then, up came two wet pink heads and the piglets started to bring their little trotters up and down in unison, going from left to right in the pond and staring at the children enthusiastically.

Celia was astounded. Like Cyril, her experience of pigs was limited to the rashers of bacon brought to her bedroom by her maidservant in the mornings. 'Can all pigs do synchronised swimming?' she asked innocently.

'No,' said Megsie, and then started to laugh. The piglets were so comical in the water. Vincent giggled and Celia giggled and soon everyone was just enjoying the show. Then, just as suddenly as they had started, the piglets swam elegantly to the other side of the pond, got out, shook themselves like a couple of dogs and ran off. Megsie groaned through her laughter.

'We've *got* to catch them!' she said, and once again, the three children raced off in hot pursuit.

Now all the piglets were heading in the same direction, and Norman and Cyril reached the top of a little hill at exactly the same time as Celia, Megsie and Vincent. Everyone started babbling at once about what they'd seen when Vincent suddenly shouted, 'Look!'

Everyone turned. There, on the very top of the hill, were the piglets, all seven of them. They were flying in formation around the old cherry tree, looking for all the world like a carousel at a funfair but with NOTHING HOLDING THEM UP.

'They're flying!' said Vincent.

Awed and thrilled, the children approached the carousel of pigs and watched and clapped. Then Norman said, out of the corner of his mouth, 'Listen, everyone. Get in a circle round the tree. When I say the word, grab them!'

The children began to encircle the tree. The

piglets were having such a good time flying that they didn't appear to notice. But just at the moment when Norman hissed, 'Now!' they all dropped to the ground and ran off gleefully, giving no one the chance to catch even one of them. Norman was getting frustrated.

'How on earth are we going to catch them now? They can fly, they can swim and they can climb trees – we're done for! What am I going to tell Mum?'

Everyone went very quiet. The piglets had been wonderful to watch, it was true, but if it meant that they couldn't be caught, the situation was serious indeed. Cyril had been thinking. He was also scratching in the mud with a stick.

'What we need are tactics,' he said importantly. 'A movement order. A plan.'

'Oh yes?' said Norman sarcastically. 'And where did you learn tactics then?'

'Cadet school,' said Cyril.

'Oh,' said Norman. 'Fair enough. Let's hear it then.'

So Cyril proceeded to outline his plan . . .

The Diary

Still hotter than Hades. Talking of Hades, an odd coincidence in our world is that Ralph Fiennes is playing Hades in the next-door stage in *The Clash of the Titans*. I am going to visit. Ralph is playing our Lord Gray later in the shoot. Am very curious to see his Hades costume. Liam Neeson is also in it, giving his Zeus. Blimey. Grand or what?

Later: Have been next door to visit the Titans. They are all in an excessive amount of plastic armour and woollens and nearly dead from the heat. They don't have enough air conditioning and what's more, they are shooting Olympus and the entire set is floodlit and dotted with actual flaming torches. I've never seen hotter actors in my life. Plus, this week is set to be the hottest for many years. It's 32°C in London! Great. Thanks, O Weather Gods.

I am too exhausted and sweaty to write much.

Next day: Still hotter. We can't work in the make-up room any more – it's like a sauna and all the make-up comes off as it goes on. They've moved downstairs. Air-con units are sprouting up everywhere, like mushrooms. I visited Titans in full costume and gave Ralph my ear lobes. We are going to do a new film called *Clash of Nanny McPhee and the Titans*. Nanny McPhee will be Hades's girlfriend. Ralph has a big pretend forehead, so we think they will suit each other.

We are mopping up some unfinished scenes, which is very confusing. Lots of long discussions about who is looking where and when and what they were doing when we shot the first bit and so forth. Many people scratching heads and looking thoroughly flummoxed. Even Irene, who is never flummoxed. Quite funny really. Except not.

Was walking down the corridor to the set when I heard a weird noise behind me. Like a collection of Tupperware being banged together. Turned round and it was Apollo. Any time I get the chance I go upstairs and disrobe and lie in front of my little air-con unit. Toby, our wonderful Movement Director (see Glossary), came in rather suddenly and found me naked except for my nose, boots and hat. He took it quite calmly, all things considered.

The Story

Mrs Green was dashing up the lane to the farm, hoping to get there before Farmer Macreadie came to buy the piglets. She was talking to herself: 'So. We sell the piglets. I take the money and pay for the tractor and if there's any extra – well, Vinnie needs new wellies because his are too small and Megsie's old ones are too big at the minute and Norman needs new – new everything, oh dear, perhaps we'll just make a cake.'

She reached the gate and went straight into the barn to check that the piglets were fed and watered. But the sty was empty. Mrs Green said, 'No', and, 'No, that's not right.' She looked and looked. But it was empty. She looked every-where – and thinking that they must have all escaped into the barn, she looked inside all the nooks and crannies, inside the old watering cans and under the Scratch-O-Matic, making little noises of distress. All of a sudden Phil walked in, carrying his contract.

'How's my gorgeous sister-in-law?' he said cheerily.

Mrs Green, who had got into the sty, looked up from behind the trough with a face as grey as putty.

'There's a hole,' she whispered. 'Someone's dug a hole. They're not here. They've all escaped.'

'Oh no,' said Phil, putting down the contract and pretending to look for the piglets. Because of course it was he who had dug the hole. It was he who had let out the piglets and who now hoped to get Mrs Green to sign his papers so that he could save his skin. You knew that.

The sound of hoofs was heard in the yard and a shout of 'Ahoy!' from Farmer Macreadie. Mrs Green went weak in the legs.

'Oh no. What are we going to do? How are we going to pay for the tractor?'

Farmer Macreadie walked in and immediately saw that something was badly wrong. As Mrs

Green explained, he shook his head sadly and said he'd try to help — but of course both his boys were off in the war too and he had his own fields to harvest and his own tractor to pay for. Regretfully, he started back to his horse and cart.

'Terrible thing, war,' said Phil. 'Curse these flat feet! . . .' And he tried to look frustrated about not being able to fight with all the others.

As soon as Farmer Macreadie had left the barn, Phil grabbed the contract and thrust it under Mrs Green's nose.

'Izzy, sign it, look! Sign it! One little signature and all your problems will be solved! No more worrying about tractors, no more worrying about harvests, no more worrying about —'

But his last word was cut off by a great cry from Farmer Macreadie.

'Pigs,' he cried. 'Pigs!'

Mrs Green and Phil stared at each other and ran out to see what was happening.

Farmer Macreadie was sitting in his cart at the gate to the farm and pointing and laughing and clapping at the five chattering, filthy, cheering children who were now making their way into the yard with seven exhausted piglets in their arms. Vincent's were on leads made out of Megsie's hair ribbons. It was a wonderful sight. Nanny McPhee was at the kitchen door, a little smile playing about her mouth.

There was much laughing and shouting as they all put the piglets into the back of the cart and Farmer Macreadie, greatly relieved and happy for Mrs Green, paid her the money. Cyril caught sight of what he was handing over and ran up.

'They're worth a lot more than that!' he cried. 'These pigs can swim – and fly – and climb trees!'

Farmer Macreadie fell about laughing.

'No, no, it's true!' cried all the children. 'They can make a carousel and they can dive and do the breaststroke!'

'And synchronised swimming!' added Celia.

Mrs Green regarded them all rather sternly and said, 'Now, now. That's one thing we don't do in this family. We don't tell fibs. What will Farmer Macreadie think of us?'

But Farmer Macreadie was laughing so hard he was doubled over.

'Synch— synchronised – oh give over!' he kept saying.

Nanny McPhee came up, smiling at the children.

'But it's true!' yelled Vincent.

'Stop that now, Vinnie,' said Mrs Green.

'Leave him be, Mrs Green,' said Farmer Macreadie, wiping his eyes. 'He's just trying to get a bit more for them, and why not, eh?'

So saying, he pulled out his wallet once again and handed Mrs Green a bit extra. Then he got into the cart, and amidst much waving and shouting, drove off still giggling to himself about pigs doing synchronised swimming, which was the funniest thing he had ever heard, but you have to understand that he didn't get out much.

'Isn't it wonderful, Phil?' said Mrs Green, turning to show Phil the money – but he was no longer there.

Nanny McPhee smiled at her. 'I am happy to say, Mrs Green, that Lesson Three – to help each other – is complete,' she said.

'Oh, how wonderful!' said Mrs Green, staring rather hard at Nanny McPhee, who somehow didn't seem quite so ugly today. Perhaps it had been the storm last night that made her look so threatening. At any rate, she certainly looked much better on a sunny day. Mrs Green turned to the triumphant children.

'You are the best pig-catchers in all the –' she stopped. She walked up to Celia, who was covered in mud. She stared at her with a little frown.

'Is that my wedding dress?' she asked finally.

Celia looked down at her toes, deeply ashamed.

'I'm very sorry –' she began.

But Megsie then interrupted. 'It was our fault, Mum! We spoilt all her clothes and she had to wear something!'

Mrs Green stayed very still.

'Where's the veil?' she asked.

Cyril was holding the veil, but where once it had been a lovely white gauzy thing, it was torn and tattered and grimy in his hands like an old bit of unravelled bandage. Mrs Green walked over and took it from him.

'I'm sorry too,' said Cyril, meaning it. 'It's just that we needed a net. To catch the piglets with.

We put apples down and they came to eat them and we threw the net – I mean, the veil – over them and they couldn't get out.'

There was a pause during which all the children wondered how they were going to be punished for having done such a dreadful thing to something so precious. Mrs Green looked at their stricken faces and then did something very brave. She swallowed her upset and her anger and she put a huge smile on her face, which took a lot of effort.

'Well I never!' she said. 'What an incredibly clever thing to do! You've saved the harvest, my

darlings! Let's have a picnic to celebrate! We'll do it tomorrow and we'll use the extra pennies for ginger beer!'

And everyone cheered and cheered.

You see, parents are very annoying a lot of the time, but they are great when they do things like that. I hope you are proud of Mrs Green, because I am.

Anyway, just at that moment, when the children were all happy and friendly together, the Rolls-Royce purred up to the gate. No one had heard it approaching, what with all the excitement, but there it was. Celia yelped with amazed delight. But Norman noticed that Cyril's mouth suddenly turned downward and he frowned.

Celia was overcome with ecstasy. She jumped up and down and clapped her hands and said proudly to everyone, 'Look! It's Mummy. I told you she'd come! Mummy!' she cried. 'You'll never guess what!' and she ran up to the passenger door of the Rolls to tell her mother about the morning's adventures.

'We rescued these little piggies, and I wore wellingtons, and I ran about in the grass and everything but I got a bit dirty, I hope you won't mind – look!'

Celia threw open the door. But there was no one there.

'Mummy?' she said, in a very small voice.

Blenkinsop, his uniform cleaned and ironed (or maybe he had two – who's to know?) stepped up to Celia.

'Her Ladyship is still in London, Miss Celia,' he said.

'Oh. I suppose she's sent you to bring me home,' said Celia, smiling uncertainly at the group behind her.

'Regretfully not, Miss Celia,' said Blenkinsop, thoroughly discomfited. 'My only instructions was to bring you these pumps what you left behind. Fontarelli, I believe.'

Blenkinsop handed Celia a pretty box. She took it without a word and, in order to disguise the fact that she was crying, held it high over her face and walked away. Just as she reached the gate, she threw the box into a pile of mud. And then she was gone. There was one of those dreadfully uncomfortable silences. Cyril looked at the faces around him and felt that they were

pitying his sister. It made him very angry to think that, so, when Norman came forward and rather tentatively said, 'Cyril –' he flew off the handle.

'We're not some kind of freak show!' he shouted. 'Just leave us alone! You don't know anything about us!' And he marched off to find Celia.

'Oh dear,' said Mrs Green.

'I'd best be off, ma'am,' said Blenkinsop, his face a picture of misery.

'Oh no, Mr Blenkinsop, can't you stay for a cup of tea at least? It's a long journey back,' Mrs Green said kindly.

But Blenkinsop shook his head.

'It's not that I don't want to,' he explained glumly. 'It's just . . .'

Mrs Green knew. If he stopped even for a glass of water Lady Gray would have his guts for garters. Mrs Green nodded and the children waved him off, feeling rather sorry for him even though he got to drive such a dramatic vehicle. Mrs Green went off to pay up the tractor money, leaving the others in a sombre mood despite the morning's triumph. Megsie wandered over to the big pile of mud and picked up the dirty shoebox.

Vincent went into the barn and found Cyril loitering by the Scratch-O-Matic, looking sulky.

'I could scratch you if you like,' said Vincent helpfully. But Cyril was in no mood to be helped by anyone and he stalked out of the barn with a curt 'No, thanks' to Vincent, who shrugged and got on to the machine sadly, since there were no longer any piglets to scratch.

Back in the house, Megsie had gone up to the bedroom to change her wet socks. She found Celia sitting on the edge of the bed. Celia had been crying, she knew, and was refusing to look at her. She stood at the door and thought for a moment. Then she came forward with the shoebox.

'I picked this up,' she said. 'I thought you might want them.'

Celia sniffed. 'I don't care for them. You can have them if you like,' she said carelessly.

Now Megsie was quite a wise person. She knew fine well that Celia was only behaving in that way because she was hurt, and everyone had seen her getting hurt, which is always unpleasant. So she realised that Celia probably didn't mean it about her having the shoes. But she had never seen a fancy pair of shoes and she was very curious about them. So she sat down on the bed near Celia, but not too near, and opened the box. She couldn't help gasping when she found what was underneath the cerise tissue paper. A pair of pink pumps, so dainty, so elegant, the sort of thing a young Cinderella would have worn before the Ugly Sisters came along. They were patent leather and they glowed in Megsie's hands like a sunset. Celia glanced at Megsie's rapt face. It made her feel better to think that Megsie liked the shoes.

'No, really,' she said. 'You can keep them.'

This time, Megsie heard something in Celia's voice that meant she really *could* keep them and that Celia wasn't just saying it. She thought for a moment and then stood up and opened the little chest that she kept her best things in. She got out her new corduroy trousers, a present from her parents last Christmas, and her Sunday shirt, which had embroidery on the collar. She went back and placed them next to Celia.

'These are my best,' she said. 'But you're used to smart things so you can have them for every day.'

Celia looked at her. They gave each other a small smile.

Meanwhile, the person feeling the saddest of all about the piglets was marching into the village with a face like thunder. Phil was furious. Curse those children! They'd undone his plan and rendered his night's digging useless! He was getting more and more frightened about Miss Topsey and Miss Turvey coming back and carrying out their threat. Removing his kidneys! But he needed them! They processed waste products out of his body and were vital to sustain life!! He gulped as he walked and gnashed his teeth when he thought of how close he'd been to persuading Isabel to sign. He felt as though he were living in one of those nightmares that you can't wake yourself from.

Just as he passed the alley where he'd first met the ladies, he heard a little 'oo-oo' noise, like a cuckoo. He froze. He looked to the right and to the left. Nothing. He looked in front and behind. Again, nothing. Then he heard the noise again, above him. He looked up, half expecting to see Miss Topsey and Miss Turvey hanging from the tree branches like a couple of gigantic, blood-sucking bats. But there, in the tree, was a lovely little bird, its head cocked to one side as it sang 'oo-oo' sweetly at him. Phil gave a sob of relief and turned back, walking straight into the majestic bosom of Miss Turvey.

'Hello, Phil,' she said. 'Have you missed me?'

The Diary

We've been shooting in the bedroom today. It's upstairs. It is therefore higher up than the kitchen set and, as you all know, heat rises. It is sunny. All the lamps are on. It is 44°C up there. The crew are all pink and panting, and the children, who are in pyjamas and

under bedclothes have to be sponged down at regular intervals. I am in full costume so I won't even tell you what it's like in there, except to say that it smells like something died.

I discovered that one of our excellent Runners (see Glossary), whom I have been calling Lauren for the past few weeks, is in fact called Laura.

'Why didn't you tell me?' I shriek, aghast.

'Because it doesn't matter and you've got far too much else to remember,' she replied smartly and without fuss. You see why one loves a crew. They work until they drop and then they say things like that. Amazing.

Later: We've finished in the bedroom and have moved on to another stage to do a bit of 'green screen'. This is where you have to shoot something in front of a lot of green and then stuff is laid into the background by the FX team. In this instance, it is the fabulous Rolls-Royce (which costs £1,000 per day!) and Celia and Cyril doing a vomming scene, which they perform to comic and emotional perfection every time. They really are extraordinary, the pair of them. We're packing up here at Shepperton because the next bit of the shoot is happening outside again, on a whole new location. It renders the place a bit like old digs at the end of a theatre job – full of boxes and cases (mostly my noses) and all the comforts of life packed away. Bit depressing, really, but we get a week off and then we go outside, which could be uplifting, depending on the weather. You can't win. As soon as you go inside the studio, it gets hot and lovely outside. As soon as you leave studio, it starts to rain. It's just what happens. Every. Single. Time. Ask Lindsay.

The Titans have packed up and left too, which is very sad. No more gold and silver Tupperware . . .

The Story

Phil gaped at Miss Turvey in complete horror as Miss Topsey appeared from behind her and gave one of her silvery laughs.

'Oh, Phil, we are sorry, we didn't mean to frighten you!' she trilled.

'I'm getting it! I'm getting the farm for you, I just need a signature, ladies, please understand that I'm getting it and I *will* get it and then *you* will get it, please – there's no need for –'

'For what, Phil?' asked Miss Topsey, looking genuinely mystified.

'For what you said – my kidneys –'

'Oh that!' said Miss Topsey, waving her hand as if to dismiss the whole kidney affair altogether.

'Oh, don't worry about that, Phil, we're not going to take your kidneys off you! For heaven's sake! Who do you think we are?'

Phil sagged against Miss Turvey's bosom with relief. She lifted him away and propped him against the tree. Then she leaned in and said, 'We've come up with a much better idea, Phil.'

'Much better!' agreed Miss Topsey, clapping her hands with delight.

Nanny McPhee (Emma Thompson) and her mischievous jackdaw, Mr Edelweiss.

Celia Gray (Rosie Taylor-Ritson) will not get out of the car at her cousins' farm, despite the attempts of her chauffeur (Daniel Mays).

Nanny McPhee and Mr Edelweiss inside the Greens' farmhouse.

Nanny McPhee surveys the Greens' farm.

Cyril Gray (Eros Vlahos) brandishes the Green children's special pot of strawberry jam.

The five cousins run after the escaped piglets. From left to right: Vincent (Oscar Steer), Celia, Cyril, Norman (Asa Butterfield) and Megsie (Lil Woods).

Norman and Cyril, with the help of Vincent, prepare to catch the escaped piglets with Mrs Green's wedding veil.

The cousins triumphantly return to the farm, having found all the escaped pigs. From left to right: Norman, Cyril, Megsie, Vincent and Celia.

A prize piglet!

Phil (Rhys Ifans) gets ready to perform a dastardly deed.

Fighting cousins. From left to right: Norman scuffles with Cyril while Megsie takes on Celia.

Vincent operating the Scratch-O-Matic, a custom-built animal scratcher.

Mrs Green (Maggie Gyllenhaal) hangs up her wedding veil to dry.

The unexploded bomb in the barley field. Looking on, from left to right: Nanny McPhee, Celia, Cyril, Norman, Mrs Green and Megsie.

From left to right: Cyril, Norman and Mrs Green watch in wonder as a magical event unfurls in their barley field.

'Hold this, Phil,' said Miss Turvey, opening her vast handbag and handing him a flat thing about the size of a chessboard covered with pretend grass. Phil held it, his heart beating double time and his knees shaking uncontrollably. Next, Miss Turvey took out a little figure in a blue suit – it had Phil's hair and Phil's shoes and Phil's tie, all tiny and very accurately drawn.

'Look!' said Miss Topsey. 'It's you! Do you see, Phil?'

Phil nodded uncertainly. What on earth were they doing?

'And look! What's this?'

She opened her bag and took out a toy tractor.

'It's a tractor,' said Phil, staring at the little figure on the grassy board with increasing dread.

'And now look – what's happening? You're going for a nice walk in the country!'

Miss Topsey walked the little figure along the grass and Miss Turvey moved the tractor towards it, making engine noises and smiling encouragingly at Phil.

'Choof-choof-choof-choof, see? And see what happens!'

Miss Turvey rolled the toy tractor over the little figure as both the ladies made terrible cracking noises and its legs and arms and head came off. Phil watched. The ladies looked at him joyfully.

'We're going to squash you with farm machinery!' they chorused.

Not knowing quite how, Phil staggered away down the lane, shouting, 'Now there's no need for that, there's no need!' as the ladies called out after him: 'Better hurry, Phil! Before it's too late!'

'How will I know when it's too late?' shrieked Phil, from the safety of a ditch.

The two hit-women looked at each other

and then back at Phil. 'We'll send a sign,' they shouted, waving cheerily.

Chapter Quobbly. I realise that I've been rather lax about the whole chapter thing, so here's one with an exciting new number to it. One might as well be creative, don't you think?

Anyway, it's the next day.

It was a beautiful morning and the children had managed to rub along with each other fairly well except for Cyril, who was still sulking. He wasn't entirely sure why he was sulking, but no one had given him any real reason to leave off so he just carried on. This is the problem with sulking, I find. The difficulty is never in starting it but in stopping it, because I suddenly feel a bit daft, which makes me feel cross, which starts me off wanting to sulk all over again.

Mrs Green had made a big picnic as promised and had invited Mrs Docherty and Mr Spolding who was still carrying his pamphlette. There were sandwiches (bloater paste and egg-and-cress because bloater paste was cheap and they got eggs free from the chickens) and apples and one large bottle of ginger beer, which Vincent was so excited about that he hadn't slept a wink all night.

The party set out in glorious sun and found a perfect spot – good slopes for rolling down, a nice flat bit for the blanket and some pasture for the goat, whom they'd brought along to eat any leftovers. Everyone had made an effort. Mrs Docherty had a felt flower in her hat, Mr Spolding had polished his buttons and tucked in his string vest, Mrs Green was wearing her best Sunday dress and Nanny McPhee was sporting a very impressive row of medals on her chest about which the children were very curious. Everyone but Cyril was in a good mood, and Nanny McPhee hadn't even objected when the children had, rather timidly, asked if they might invite Mr Edelweiss. They were also curious about Mr Edelweiss and Nanny McPhee, but they didn't speak jackdaw and Nanny McPhee simply wasn't the sort of person you asked intimate questions. She just wasn't.

But after everyone (except Cyril) had had a game of cricket and done lots of cartwheels and had a sandwich and an apple, Mr Edelweiss came quite close to Megsie and accepted a crumb out of her hand.

Nanny McPhee tutted and said, 'Get away with you, Mr Edelweiss, you greedy bird.'

Megsie decided to risk it.

'Why do you call him Mr Edelweiss, Nanny McPhee?'

Nanny McPhee looked at the children, who were sitting in a sort of circle before her (except Cyril, who was a metre to the left). 'Well,' she said, 'the edelweiss, as you know, is a small white flower and he is a large black bird!'

I don't know whether Nanny McPhee thought this was a good joke but the children certainly didn't so they just kept on staring at her politely as if there was going to be more.

Nanny McPhee sniffed. 'It was funny at the time,' she said apologetically. At that moment Mr Edelweiss let out a very loud burp which all the children (except Cyril) thought *was* funny.

'Don't be so disgusting,' said Nanny McPhee sternly.

'What's he done to make you so cross with him?' asked Norman.

Everyone sat up and paid special attention now. Mr Edelweiss burped again but tried to cover it with a cough.

'He eats inappropriate substances. Such as window putty.'

Here, Mr Edelweiss uttered a single guilty and slightly burpy squawk and took a step away from the group.

'Such as . . .' continued Nanny McPhee, fixing Mr Edelweiss with one of her beadiest looks, 'such as all the window putty off every single one of my window panes, which all fell out when the bishop came to tea!'

'That's really bad,' muttered Megsie.

Everyone looked at Mr Edelweiss now. He hopped off yet further, squawking and burping in a depressed and almost whiny way.

'What's he saying?' asked Celia.

'You really don't want to know,' said Nanny McPhee, sighing heavily.

Anxious to change a subject so clearly painful to the parties involved, Celia decided to pay Nanny McPhee a compliment.

'You are looking well today, I must say, Nanny McPhee,' she said.

'Thank you, dearie,' said Nanny McPhee with a little smile. The children noticed that she really was looking better – they couldn't quite say how, but she certainly wasn't quite so ugly any more. It was very odd.

'I think it's the country air,' said Celia. 'My skin's better too.'

'What are your medals for, Nanny McPhee?' said Norman.

Nanny McPhee looked down at her chest and, pointing to each one in turn, said, 'Courage. Kindness. Resolve. Imagination. Enthusiasm. Basketwork and Leaps of Faith.'

They all nodded, highly impressed.

At that moment, Mr Spolding made a huge exploding noise. Everyone looked over. He was pretending to be a bomb.

'BOOFBANGBIFFBOOFBOOF!' he shouted, going very pink in the face. 'You see, Mrs Green? There's a war on and that's the sort of fatalistic explosion that could happen any second of the moment! That's what you people don't seem to understand! And that's why I'm here – to protect you from yourselves!'

'That's enough now, Algernon,' said Mrs Docherty, who understood Mr Spolding very well.

'So,' said Mr Spolding, taking no notice of anyone at all, 'if a bomb drops, let me know as soon as possible!'

'You'll probably notice all by yourself, Mr Spolding,' said Mrs Green kindly. 'Anyway, guess what! It's time for ginger beer!'

Vincent let out a huge whoop, which was echoed by all the other children (except Cyril) as they ran up to Mrs Green and queued with their tumblers for the precious treat. Vincent got his first and went and sat on the very far edge of the blanket so that no one could jog him or ask him for a sip because they'd gulped theirs down too quickly. You remember what I told you about Vincent and his chocolate bars and how long he could make them last. Well, he planned to make this little glass of ginger beer last right up until bedtime. He watched it for a bit and smelt it and then looked up and far away so that he could forget about it and then get a lovely surprise. While he was busy forgetting, he caught sight of a familiar blue suit walking along the edge of the field.

'Here's Uncle Phil!' he cried. 'Quick! Finish the buns!'

It wasn't that Vincent was being mean or even that he didn't like his uncle. He did. It was just that everyone was used to the fact that you could rely on Uncle Phil to turn up just when a cake was being taken out of the oven or when a bottle of something nice was being opened.

Mrs Green shielded her eyes against the sun and said, 'He's never normally late when there are treats. Here he is though – with his bloomin' contract.' But she said the bit about the contract under her breath.

But as Phil got closer it became clear that it wasn't the contract he was carrying, it was something much smaller. Mrs Green narrowed her eyes, 'Ooh!' she said excitedly. 'It's not the contract, it's too small – it must be a letter!'

Vincent jumped up, taking great care not to spill his ginger beer.

Now everyone gathered to watch Phil approaching. Mr Spolding leaned over to Mrs Docherty and said, 'A letter from Rory – won't that be nice, after all their waiting?'

But Mrs Docherty was gazing anxiously into his eyes. 'Didn't you see, Algernon? It's yellow,' she whispered. 'That's not a letter. That's a telegram.'

Mr Spolding went white. He took Mrs Docherty's hand and together they watched as Phil came up to Mrs Green and the waiting children.

I can't be sure quite when Mrs Green and the children realised that the thing Phil was holding was yellow. It was one of those moments when something you don't want to happen happens and everything slows down. To Vincent, and Megsie, and Norman, it certainly seemed to

take Phil a long, long time to reach them. When he did, finally, Vincent just said, very quietly, 'That's not for us, is it?'

Phil didn't speak. He looked awful. He handed Mrs Green the telegram without a word. Mrs Green looked at all the stricken faces and said, 'It's not always bad news, my darlings. He might have got a medal!'

But she knew she had to open it. So she did. Almost immediately everyone knew that Mr Green hadn't won a medal and that it was the worst news ever. Mrs Green didn't cry or scream or anything. She just said, 'Oh,' and sank to her knees. Vincent dropped his ginger beer on the ground and rushed to bury his head in her lap. Norman picked up the telegram, read it and then put it down, walking away from everyone towards the farm. Megsie picked it up and read the words: 'RORY GREEN. KILLED IN ACTION. DEEPEST CONDOLENCES'. She wrapped herself silently around her mother. Phil bent his head and leant by Mrs Green's side, tears in his eyes. Very slowly, Mrs Docherty, Mr Spolding and Nanny McPhee started to clear up the picnic things. Celia helped, hardly daring to look at the family. Cyril, having finally found a very good reason to stop sulking, watched it all with a heavy heart and finally decided to follow Norman.

The Diary

We're on location at Wormsley! The barley field! Thirty acres of it! We're not allowed to walk on it. Once again, the call-sheet is covered with huge supplications like 'PLEASE PLEASE PLEASE DON'T WALK ON THE BARLEY!!' and 'IT TOOK US EIGHT MONTHS TO GROW THE BARLEY. IF YOU STEP ON IT WE CANNOT REPAIR THE DAMAGE!!' and so forth. It is the most beautiful location I have ever seen – a great rippling field of stalks that change colour as they move and make the most wonderful susurrations. Sometimes it even sounds like it's sighing to itself. Right in the middle is the pretend bomb, which is huge. Since we all have to go and act in and around the bomb, they have built a walkway to it – so if you stand on the edge of the field and look across it looks as if people are floating over the top of the barley. Magical. The Art Department are going to hand-harvest this crop on Saturday in readiness for the harvest sequences. Eric is on set today, and he and I are trying to persuade them to make beer out of the barley. It seems they are going to sell it on the open market – people make things out of unprocessed barley and it's used in thatching as well. They think the field is worth about £8,000!! Any money they get will go back into the production. Lindsay thinks beer is a bad idea, but she's American and I'm sure not how attractive the prospect of home-brew is for her . . .

The children and Maggie Smith, who is playing Mrs Docherty, are running through the barley and it looks wonderful, but is full of sharp FLINTS, and they've all got sore knees from falling. It is a wonderful location, but you can't get in and out of it very easily. So we get to our positions and then have to stay there for most of the day. We do have little boxes to sit on, but Maggie is not in the first flush of youth and nor am I and it's not easy to sit in a blinking field all day. The ADs yell instructions at us from over the top of yards of unspoilt barley. They're all getting hoarse. We hide our water bottles among the barley stalks, and if I get too hot I take off my boots and stand on them. No one can see my feet, after all.

Oooh. Just seen the bomb shuddering and letting off

steam. It's very impressive and really quite scary. This is a very difficult bit to shoot. We have to do all the scenes out of order so that we only squash the right bits of the barley at the right time and in the right order. Eeek. It's taken them the entire week off to work out the shot lists, so all I can say is thank God Rhys broke his foot.

Gaia is now on set and working as a Runner. She's very efficient. Last night we went back to the hotel and had room service and watched penguins on the telly.

The Story

Cyril was feeling perfectly dreadful. Now his sulk was over, he was able to think about his own behaviour in relation to this nice family who had taken him in, and he wasn't enjoying it at all. Why had he been so awful on that first day? He'd been feeling very sick because of the journey and all the chocolate he'd eaten – and come to that, why had he eaten all the chocolate? He decided it was because it made him feel better while it was in his mouth but worse when it reached his tummy. And then he'd broken the jam they'd made for their father, and now he was dead, and Cyril's conscience was giving Cyril a very hard time of it. He knew he had to do something, he just didn't know what. He'd followed Norman instinctively, but had no idea what he would do when he found him. He searched the house but Norman wasn't there. Then Cyril realised where he'd be. He walked into the barn and sure enough, there was Norman, sitting on the Scratch-O-Matic with his back to him. Cyril stopped and thought. What do you say when someone's just found out that their dad isn't going to come home ever? What if he was crying? Then Cyril remembered what Prongwithers Minor had come up with when Cyril's grandmother had died last term.

'Rotten luck,' he said.

Norman turned and looked at him briefly, then turned back, not rudely but as if he were concentrating on something.

Cyril saw that he wasn't crying and also that he wasn't angry with Cyril – so he decided to try something more difficult. He tried to apologise.

'Look, I'm sorry,' he said, 'about the way I've

been – I don't know why I . . . anyway, I'm sorry.'

'Doesn't matter. Forget it,' said Norman, and Cyril knew he meant it.

Cyril felt a bit better and walked around to look at the levers of the wonderful machine Mr Green had invented. Tactfully he concentrated on the machine and not on Norman.

'This is a great idea,' he said. 'He's . . . He must've been a brilliant designer, your dad –'

Norman interrupted him. 'He's not dead,' he said.

Cyril was so surprised that he turned to look straight at Norman.

'What?' he said.

'He's not dead. I know it. For sure.' And Norman did look very sure.

'Norman, how do you know?' said Cyril, worried that Norman might have gone temporarily insane, like his Aunt Jemima when she'd found a weevil in the pistachios.

Norman looked at Cyril for a long time, rather intensely, as though trying to make a decision. It was starting to make Cyril feel very uncomfortable when suddenly Norman spoke again, as if he'd decided to trust Cyril somehow.

'My dad's more than just a farmer. My dad's what they call a natural. That means that he knows when things are going to happen – he knows when the cow's going to calve or when a lamb's in trouble on the hill. He says it's because he feels things in his bones. And he's always right. Always. Well, I can feel it in my bones that he's alive. I just know it.'

Cyril was silent for a bit. He was thinking furiously. Norman seemed utterly certain of what he'd just said. Cyril could see from the firm, clear gaze in Norman's eyes that he was sure his father was alive. What did one do in such a situation? Nothing in cadet school had prepared him for this.

Very gently, he started to speak, 'Norman, are you sure you don't feel like this because – well – because you've just heard and –'

Cyril was about to suggest that Norman couldn't face the truth, but Norman cut him off again, forcefully but kindly.

'No, no. I know that's what it looks like, but no. I just know.'

'But the telegram –' said Cyril.

174

'They've got it wrong,' said Norman.

Cyril was appalled. He swallowed before he spoke.

'Norman, the War Office doesn't get that kind of thing wrong.'

'They've got it wrong,' repeated Norman.

It was very hard for Cyril to accept that the War Office, the place where his father worked, would ever get anything wrong, but Norman was so clear and so certain that Cyril found even his faith wavering. He sat down on a bale of straw.

'All right,' he said. 'What do you want to do about it?'

Norman looked at Cyril and smiled.

'I need some tactics, Cyril.'

Now Cyril grinned.

'I need to get to the War Office and find out what's happened to my father.'

'Why don't you just tell your mother about all this?' asked Cyril.

'Because she won't believe me. She'll believe the telegram. It's not her fault; she just doesn't feel things in the same way. And this is too big – I've got to bring her proof. And I've got to do it fast, otherwise she'll sell the farm to Uncle Phil, I know she will. She'll think we can't manage it on our own.'

Cyril saw the wisdom of this immediately. In his experience, grown-ups never believed anything a child said ever, and so he started to work out how on earth Norman was going to achieve what he needed to achieve.

'Trouble is,' continued Norman, 'I can't very well go off looking for him, can I? We don't even know what country he's in!'

'There might be a way,' said Cyril doubtfully.

Norman looked at him sharply. 'What?'

'Well . . . my father – he's very high up in the War Office . . .'

'So you've said,' said Norman wryly.

'Thing is, I think he'd be able to find out.'

'Of course!' said Norman excitedly. 'Where's the War Office exactly?'

'London,' said Cyril.

'How are we going to get in touch with him? Could we send him a letter?'

'He doesn't respond to letters. At least, not to mine,' said Cyril.

'Think!'

'Norman, I don't know. We wouldn't be allowed to travel on a train without tickets, and I don't have any money and nor do you.'

'We're going to need help.'

'Who can help us?'

'Who?'

Then the boys heard a very strange thing – it was as though they were in a tunnel and their voices were echoing back at them. All they could hear was 'Help us, help us, help us . . .' whispered back at them over and over. There was a sharp bang and the noises stopped. The boys whirled in the direction of the bang, and there was Nanny McPhee, looking in at them from the barn door.

'You called?' she said.

The boys looked at one another in amazement. Then they ran over to Nanny McPhee.

'Nanny McPhee, Dad's alive – I can feel it in my bones, but I've got to bring Mum proof before she'll believe it. Can you help us?'

It didn't occur to Norman or to Cyril that this statement would not be believed. But Nanny McPhee was not like other grown-ups. Not at all.

'Help you in what way?' said Nanny McPhee.

'We need to reach Cyril's father!' said Norman.

'Yes!' said Cyril. 'My father's Lord Gray – he's very high up in –'

'I know who he is,' said Nanny McPhee politely.

'Yes, well, anyway, he can help us find out about Uncle Rory – could you help us to contact him?'

'I fear that would be difficult. Lord Gray is a very important man, and I am of little consequence to him.'

Norman and Cyril looked at each other in consternation.

'Then can you help us to get to him in London?' said Norman.

'Help two unaccompanied children to travel to London?' said Nanny McPhee, looking grave. 'I fear that would be very much against army regulations.' And she turned and started to walk away.

Norman looked defeated. 'Then how will we get there? What can we do?'

'I don't know,' said Cyril, helplessly.

Nanny McPhee reached the door and turned back to them. 'I said "unaccompanied",' she remarked lightly. 'You two, however, will be with me. I shall need you to be dressed warmly and ready at the duck pond just before dawn. We shall be in London by ten o'clock. Try to get the dirt out from under your nails.'

'Oh, thank you, Nanny McPhee,' breathed Norman.

'Yes, thank you!' said Cyril, feeling almost as grateful as Norman, even though it wasn't his father who might or might not be dead.

Nanny McPhee bowed graciously and led the boys back to the house.

The Diary

Everyone is very stressed by barley-squashing, which does sometimes happen accidentally, causing Lisa from the Art Department to gnash her teeth. People get shouted at – I shouted at Liam, our Set Photographer (see Glossary), when all the poor man was trying to do was get out of the way. 'You're squashing the barley, Liam!' I shrieked, and everyone looked and then I felt dreadful. And we have all discovered that hours of standing in a barley-field makes your eyes go all red and itchy. There's lots of dust from the stalks, which crumble in your hands if you roll them between your fingers (which is fun so we all do it all the time) so that must be why. But – and this is important – in spite of all the difficulties, everyone agrees that it looks quite incredible and is one of the most beautiful things they have ever seen. So it WILL all be worth it.

Maggie Smith is our hero. She skips up and down the platforms and on and off wobbling boxes like a nineteen-year-old. She and I sit for hours telling stories and roaring with dirty laughter, so it's not all bad, being in the barley. Maggie Gyllenhaal is looking after the children with immense tenderness, and Sam Kelly (our Mr Spolding) is lying down (this is the bit of the scene after Mr Spolding has fainted, you see) and being saintly, because Oscar (Vincent) keeps on tickling his nose hairs with barley stalks and laughing when he sneezes. Lil has been up the ladder for hours and is absolutely wonderful about it. Lil Woods, who plays Megsie, lives on a farm in real life, which is why you absolutely believe in her all the time. All in all, everyone is being quite remarkable. I am comfy in my costume because it is not so big and my nose is quite a sweet little buttony size now, so it doesn't come off quite as often as the big one.

The next day: Oh. I have had an allergic reaction to the barley dust and keep having to put drops in my eyes. Still, only two more days like this and then they harvest the stuff – which is rather a shame but also will help because we'll be able to get about.

Something quite funny except not really just happened. Lil was up the top of the ladder with the screwdriver, doing the bit where Megsie unscrews the cover, and she dropped the screwdriver on top of Arthur, the Boom Operator (see Glossary), and scraped his cheek. He is now wearing a hard hat, as is everyone near the bomb, because Lil has to throw the cover aside too and nearly took Darren's (the Runner's) head off with it first time. I had no idea it was all going to get so dangerous round here.

The Story

How Cyril and Norman managed to survive the evening and night without telling anyone what they were up to, I have no idea. But they did. It was, of course, an indescribably miserable evening, with Mrs Green trying desperately to be brave and behave more or less normally but unable to stop huge tears from sliding down her cheeks all the time. Nanny McPhee had a very calming influence upon Vincent, who was in a state of hysteria. Finally it was Megsie who said they should all go to bed, and Celia agreed and everyone went upstairs. Vincent slept with his mum, and Megsie cried herself to sleep with Celia lying by her, open-eyed and sleepless with the horror of it all. Finally, very early, when Celia was asleep at last, Megsie crept out and joined her mother and brother in the big bed, but she didn't notice that Cyril and Norman's bed was empty except for two pillows they'd placed under the blankets to make it look as if they were still there.

I feel I ought to say a word here about the family's reaction to the terrible news. In those days, every single person in England, whether they were rich or poor, believed that when a dreadful thing happened to you, you HAD to be brave about it. I mean, you had to try not to cry in front of people and you even had to try to be cheerful. I can't quite explain why they believed this but they did. Personally, if I'd had a day like that I'd get into bed with everyone who felt like it and sob and sob and sob until I couldn't sob any more. And I'd probably be allowed too as well, because things have changed and people don't really believe in not showing how they feel any more. Isn't it interesting, though? What would you do? Don't answer that now – we're in the middle of the story.

You don't need me to tell you that neither Cyril nor Norman slept a wink that night. Norman had a torch under the covers and checked his watch every half-hour. He wanted to get up at 2 a.m. but Cyril persuaded him, in a hissed undertone, that that would make it far more likely they'd be discovered and the plan would fail before it had even started. Finally, they rose at 4 a.m., when it was still dark, crept out with their clothes and got dressed, shiveringly, in the kitchen. Norman wrote a little note to Megsie, instructing her what to say to Mrs Green if the necessity arose, and went and hid it in the egg basket, knowing she would find it

when she got up to fetch the eggs. When he came back from the barn, there was a sliver of light on the edge of the hill, and the boys found that after all their waiting they had to hurry. They reached the duck pond and found a wonderful sight.

It was Nanny McPhee in a pair of goggles and leather gauntlets sitting astride the best vehicle they had ever seen – a khaki army-issue motorcycle complete with sidecar! It knocked the Rolls-Royce into a cocked hat! They just managed to stop themselves from whooping before Nanny McPhee kitted them out with capes and goggles of their own and hurried them into the sidecar. In great spirits and full of hope, they were off before the sun had even hit the side of the hill. No one noticed Mr Edelweiss following at a discreet distance.

Back in the farmhouse, everyone was still sound asleep. They had slept so badly it was likely that Norman and Cyril's absence would not be noticed for some time.

Meanwhile, Phil, who had also not slept, was up and about. He was getting himself ready to go and get Isabel to sign the contract. He knew that she would, now that Rory was dead. He also knew that it wasn't a very nice thing to do at such a time, but that if he didn't he too would be dead. He looked at his watch. It really was too early to knock on the door. Isabel would be so furious she might just refuse to sign it at all. And then – well, he shuddered to think about what might happen to him. He decided to bite his nails for a while until it was time.

The Diary

Very overcast today. My eyes are still sore and itchy and I am in a very bad mood. Have managed not to bite anyone's head off so far, but woe betide anyone who bounces up cheerily and says anything like 'How's it going?'.

Muddled and tired, but as Arthur, the boom operator with screwdriver scar, said to me only the other day, 'We do a knackering job, Em – what do you expect?' Thank God he didn't follow it up with 'And you're not as young as you were.' At any rate, he's quite right and one should expect to be tired, for heaven's sake. A large number of people have also had allergic reactions to the barley, so all in all, as well as being one of the most beautiful things in the world, it has caused a lot of bother.

Maggie Smith has come up with a wonderful line – trying to get Mr Spolding to come to after he's fainted, she's standing over him shrieking, 'Wake up, Algernon, wake *up*, I don't want you to miss it going off!'

And, we have just shot one of the funniest things I've ever seen: Maggie in the wind machine. When the huge wind comes to reap the barley, everyone is blown about like anything and it was Maggie's turn and she just walked into it and everything came off her head almost immediately, including parts of her wig, and, as she said afterwards, not an insignificant portion of her brain. We yelled with hysteria all the way through and then watched it on the video and yelled again. Bliss.

I've just looked at the new schedule and realised that during the next four weeks I get precisely four days off. Not to complain or anything but that's barely enough time to wash my knickers. Sigh.

The Story

For the boys, the huge excitement of getting into a motorcycle and being expertly driven through the countryside by Nanny McPhee had settled into new thoughts and cold knees. Norman was very worried about his father and equally concerned that his mother might do something rash in the face of the terrible news she'd received. Cyril was very apprehensive about visiting his father without having made a proper appointment and, as they approached the outskirts of the city, that apprehension started to congeal into fear. But then he turned and looked at Norman. They were coming up to Chelsea Bridge and Norman, who had never seen anything like it, was beginning to get excited all over again.

'Where are we?' he yelled at Cyril.

'Chelsea Bridge, of course!' shouted Cyril. 'Haven't you ever seen it before?'

'Don't be daft!' yelled Norman, his eyes shining. 'I've never even been to London before!'

When Cyril realised that Norman was seeing the bridges and statues and grand buildings of London for the first time, he began to enjoy himself more. He started to see things through Norman's eyes, and kept pointing out all the landmarks he knew. What a pleasure it was to be able to gesture at Buckingham Palace and shout, 'That's where the King lives!'

As they passed the palace, where the busbied guards stood like granite figures before the great golden gates, both the boys saw a figure on the central balcony. It was definitely a man, and he appeared to be wearing a dressing gown and a crown. As they passed, the figure seemed to get very excited. It started to jump up and down and wave. Nanny McPhee turned and gave a

delicate wave back.
The boys looked at
each other with eyes
like saucers. Appar-
ently Nanny McPhee
wasn't of quite as little
consequence as she'd
led them to believe.

From the palace they drove down Pall Mall
towards Trafalgar Square.

'This is where Nelson lives!' shouted Cyril as
they swung round the wonderful column and
the huge black lions. As the boys looked up at
the Admiral standing proud upon his pedestal,
the strangest thing occurred. The old sailor
seemed to take off his hat with his good arm
and bow in their direction. Cyril squealed with
shock and both boys whipped around to look at
Nanny McPhee. She blew a kiss at Nelson and
then waved at one of the lions, which had
woken up and roared with excitement as they
drove past. Norman couldn't stop laughing with
delight – it was all so unreal and yet absolutely
real at the same time.

★

Back at the farm, Mrs Green was lying in bed with Megsie and Vincent, who were still asleep. She looked at the ceiling and wondered why she could still do all the normal things like breathing and speaking when inside there was this terrifying black hole that was going to suck her inside out. Just then, there was a very gentle knock on the door. Mrs Green sat up as the children beside her stirred.

'Come in,' she said.

The door opened and Celia came in backwards, holding a tray.

'I thought you might like breakfast in bed,' she said kindly. The tray had a full teapot and a little jug of milk, toast and butter, boiled eggs and a mug full of wild flowers that Celia had gone out very early to pick. It looked so pretty that when Megsie and Vincent sat up it made them want to eat something from it, which was really very clever of Celia, because when you are in shock you really need to eat and you never feel like it.

'That is so beautiful,' said Mrs Green, truly touched. 'Put it here.' And she made a space in the centre of the bed. 'How lovely you've made it and how pretty everything looks! Come on, pour us a mug of tea then, Megs.'

Celia, pleased with how her offering had been received, started to leave the room, but Megsie and Mrs Green called out after her, 'Where are you going?'

'Well,' said Celia, feeling a bit embarrassed, 'I thought you might want to be just the family.'

'But you *are* family,' said Megsie. 'Come on, hop in, there's a warmy patch there.'

'Breakfast in bed,' said Vincent wonderingly. He had only ever had his breakfast in the kitchen.

Celia buttered him the biggest piece of toast and handed it to him.

'Thank you, Celia, you're very kind,' said Vincent, in such a grown-up way and such a small voice that Mrs Green had to work very hard not to burst into tears again.

'Will you stay and help us with the harvesting, Celia?' said Megsie.

'Of course I will!' said Celia. 'I'd love to!'

Mrs Green gave a little sigh. 'No harvesting for us, my darlings,' she said.

'What?' said Megsie, as she and Vincent turned to look at their mother, puzzled.

Mrs Green looked at their faces and took a deep breath.

'We can't manage this place without Dad, not really. I should have admitted it long ago. We'd never have got all that barley in, even with the tractor. Uncle Phil's got a buyer, but only if we sell right now, before harvest time –'

Vincent started to interrupt. 'Sell? What? Sell our farm?' he said, horror growing in his eyes.

'I know, I know, darling, it's horrible, but Dad would want – I mean would have wanted us to if we couldn't look after it properly and we can't –'

'No!' shouted Vincent.

'Listen, Vinnie, maybe in our new house you could have your own room!'

Mrs Green spoke as soothingly as she could, but Vincent was not to be soothed. He hurled his toast across the room and screamed out, 'I don't want my own room! I want to share with Megsie and Norman and Celia and Cyril! And I want my dad!!'

And with that he started to sob loudly and bury himself under the bedclothes. Everyone put down their cups and toast and tried to help. But Vincent was inconsolable. Finally, he flung himself out from the bed and ran out of the room.

Mrs Green looked at the girls. Megsie didn't want to add to the trouble by showing how upset she was, so she got up too and said she was going to feed the animals.

'Why don't you go with her?' Mrs Green suggested to Celia kindly. Celia ran off and Mrs Green started to clear up the breakfast things, worried that she had gone about telling the children the bad news in quite the wrong way and that it was too late to do anything about it.

Back on the motorcycle, the boys were both still shouting about Nelson when Nanny

McPhee suddenly pulled into a forecourt filled with soldiers and sandbags and came to a stop in front of the tallest building Norman had ever seen. She turned off the engine and said, 'Here we are.'

A gigantic brass sign saying 'THE WAR OFFICE' rose up before the boys, who immediately got out of the sidecar, took off their goggles and tried to straighten themselves out. Mr Edelweiss flapped up, panting, and tried to land on the handlebars but was cuffed away by Nanny McPhee, by no means pleased to see that he'd followed them. Nanny McPhee gave the boys an approving nod and they marched off towards the entrance. They could see the great main door — lots of men and women in uniform were coming in and out of it at great speed and with a tremendous sense of urgency. Norman could feel the suspense constricting his heart, and Cyril was so nervous that his mouth had gone completely dry. Just as they were about to mount the steps and go in, they found their way blocked by a gigantic soldier in red, who seemed to have come out of nowhere. Thinking he had just made a mistake, Norman tried to get past him, but he moved to block them again and both the boys realised that he was preventing them from going in on purpose. They looked up at him. His face was impassive and his eyes stared straight ahead. It was very odd. If it hadn't been for the fact that every time they tried to get around him he blocked their path, they could have sworn he hadn't even seen them. Norman nudged Cyril, who said, 'Excuse me, sir, we're here to see Lord Gray.'

The soldier did not reply and did not move. Norman decided to have a go.

'Sir – we're here to see Lord Gray!' he shouted, in case the soldier couldn't hear very well.

Then the boys heard something.

'GetlorstbeforeIthumpyer,' it sounded like. Had it come from the soldier? He hadn't budged and neither of the boys had seen his mouth move. They looked around, confused, and then it came again, louder this time.

'GET LORST BEFORE I THUMP YER,' it said, and this time Norman saw the side of the soldier's lips move slightly. He looked at Cyril worriedly.

Cyril caught the look and nodded as if he knew
what to do. 'He's my father,' he said, in that
important tone that Norman had once hated so
much but was now very grateful for.

But the soldier gave no sign of having heard.
Norman grew impatient.

'He's his FATHER,' he shouted, with all his might.

'Prove it or hop it,' said the giant.

'What?' said Cyril, suddenly feeling sick.

'PROVE IT OR HOP IT.'

Norman turned to Cyril expectantly.

'Go on, then,' he said.

Cyril had gone very pale. He drew Norman aside and said, 'How can I *prove* it? Do you carry your blinking birth certificate around with you everywhere you go? Because *I* don't!'

Norman thought. 'There must be someone inside who could say it was you,' he said.

'No, no,' said Cyril wretchedly. 'I've never even been here before – I'm not allowed.'

Norman lost his temper. 'Then why are we here? How on earth did you think we were going to get in? Why didn't we go to your house first? We're running out of time!'

Cyril started to hiss back, furious with himself, with the soldier and with Norman, when they heard a little cough behind them.

'Ahem,' it went.

They turned and there was Nanny McPhee – but so different! Gone was the rusty black cloth trimmed with jet, the black straw hat and button-boots! In their place was a full army uniform, complete with tin helmet, khaki boots and cartridge belt. The only things they recognised were the medals and, of course, the stick.

'Sergeant Jefferies,' said Nanny McPhee, looking at the enormous soldier sternly, 'you've grown.'

At the sound of her voice, an extraordinary change came over the guardsman. He gasped, stared at her, tried to bow, which caused his busby to wobble, and so instead executed a complicated series of manoeuvres with his rifle before saluting ever so smartly and saying, 'Nanny McPhee, ma'am!'

'At ease, Ralph,' said Nanny McPhee, walking up past the gaping boys and examining the sergeant more closely.

'Lesson Three paid off, I see,' she said.

'It certainly did, Nanny McPhee,' said the sergeant, looking pleased.

'How's the army treating you?'

'Proudly, ma'am, proudly!'

'I'm glad to hear it. Have you learnt to eat your greens?'

The soldier stopped looking pleased and blushed. He started to stammer and then fiddled at length with something on his rifle.

'Well?' said Nanny McPhee, mildly.

'I can't lie to you, Nanny McPhee,' he said. 'Broccoli still presents a challenge.'

The boys couldn't believe their ears.

'Try it with cheese,' said Nanny McPhee. 'And don't forget that in May and June, asparagus provides a pleasant alternative. Now. To business. I shall answer for these two boys. Please let them in at once.'

'On the double, Nanny McPhee, ma'am!' said the sergeant, coming to attention and beckoning to the boys, who sprinted up, grinning at Nanny McPhee and mouthing their thank-yous as they were marched briskly into the great building.

Meanwhile, sniffing back tears, Megsie was about to feed the chickens when she found a note in the egg basket with her name on it. She opened it, read it and gave a little shriek, which Celia, who had just walked in, heard.

'What is it?' said Celia.

'It's the boys! They've gone to London!' said Megsie.

'No! I thought they were still in bed!' said Celia, who had also been completely taken in by the pillows under the bedclothes trick.

'Look!' said Megsie, showing Celia the note.

Dad not dead. Feel it in my
bones. Don't tell Mum. Gone to
London to get proof from War
Office. Watch over farm.
Back Soon. N

Celia thought she was going to faint. 'He's not dead?' she said.

'No! If Norman can feel it in his bones, then it must be true!!' said Megsie. 'He's never wrong!'

'But your mum's just said she's going to sell the farm!' said Celia, clapping her hands to her mouth.

'We can't let her do that,' said Megsie.

'But how on earth are we going to stop her?' said Celia.

'I don't know,' said Megsie. 'But we might not have to. Norman says he'll be back soon – we'll just have to hope he gets back before she does anything! Quick! Let's get back to the house!'

Sergeant Jefferies had walked the boys through an enormous room full of maps and strange tall chairs and phones and people pushing things around on a gigantic table with wooden paddles. Everyone was concentrating terribly hard and there were a lot of quiet but urgent calls on telephones, which made Cyril feel that he really was in the centre of things and Norman feel vaguely sick because somewhere his poor father was caught up in all of it. Then they'd gone up some marble stairs and along a carpeted corridor, where all the people they passed seemed to have more stripes on their uniforms than the people they'd seen in the big map room. Then they'd turned a corner and found themselves in front of a huge door. Sergeant Jefferies had stopped, saluted the boys in formal fashion and marched away, leaving them alone.

'This must be it,' whispered Cyril.

He was terrified.

Norman said, 'Hadn't we better kno—' and at that moment, a dapper little man with a moustache opened the door and came upon them. He gave a little shriek of dismay and shock before staring at them as if they had three heads each and boils. Norman decided to get things moving.

'We're here to see Lord Gray,' he said, trying to make his voice sound important. 'Lord Gray is this person's father. It's a matter of life and death,' he added, feeling pleased that he'd sounded calm and strong. Cyril looked at him admiringly.

'Father?' said the dapper little man, looking as if he'd never heard the word before. A woman with a very large hairdo came up behind him now, saying, 'What is going on, Lieutenant Addis?'

The little man turned and waved his hands about in agitation.

'These . . . urchins say they have an appointment, Miss Spratling . . . with Lord Gray. Apparently, that boy' – the lieutenant jabbed a finger at Cyril – 'is his son. Does Lord Gray *have* children? I had no idea.'

Both Miss Spratling and Lieutenant Addis now stared at the pair as if they were museum exhibits.

'There is some resemblance in the nose area,' said Miss Spratling, examining Cyril minutely. Norman felt embarrassed and uncomfortable for Cyril. It was humiliating that these people didn't even know that he existed. Very crossly, Miss Spratling snapped at them, 'Wait here one moment, please. And don't touch anything.'

Both Miss Spratling and the lieutenant disappeared for a moment. Norman looked at Cyril, wanting to give him an encouraging smile, but Cyril seemed very far away and looked pale. There wasn't time to talk, because almost immediately Miss Spratling came back, looking harassed.

'You're to come this way,' she said, looking at the boys as if they were responsible for something rather awful and she didn't like them very much.

She led them through another office, this one a bit more normal, up to a pair of gigantic mahogany doors. She knocked gently, opened one door and pushed the boys inside, closing it quickly as though whatever was inside might grab her and bite her.

Back at the farm, Mrs Green was at the sink washing up the breakfast things and trying to swallow the rest of her tea. Suddenly, there was a sharp knock at the door and Uncle Phil walked in with the contract under his arm. Mrs Green tried to be polite.

'It's very early, Phil,' she said.

'Sorry!' said Phil, casting a terrified glance behind him, which made Mrs Green wonder what he was afraid of. (You know, of course.)

'Sorry – I know it's early. It's just that the sooner we get this done, the better!'

'Phil, just put it down and have a cup of tea, for heaven's sake,' said Mrs Green irritably. 'We'll deal with all that later.'

'No, no! It has to be now! You don't understand!' said Phil.

'No, Phil, I don't. I don't understand at all.'

'It has to be now. Else we'll lose the sale, that's all,' said Phil, trying to sound calm. 'That's all it is! We'll lose the sale if we don't sign off NOW.'

Mrs Green stared at him. He was all white and sweaty-looking as though he weren't very well. Then she reflected upon the fact that he'd just lost his brother and was entitled to be feeling all sorts of things she couldn't guess at, so she put down the tea towel and with a resigned shrug, said, 'Oh, you'd better get a pen then.'

Flooded with relief, Phil put the contract out

on the table and got out his fountain pen and unscrewed the top. Mrs Green dried her hands and came to sit down. As she started to look through the document, Megsie and Celia came hurtling indoors, stopping suddenly as they saw what was going on.

'Mum! What are you doing?!' said Megsie, utterly aghast.

'You know what I'm doing, darling,' said Mrs Green. 'It's what we talked about this morning.'

'But, Mum! You can't sign anything without waiting for Norman!'

'Where *is* Norman, actually?' said Mrs Green. 'And Cyril – they can't still be in bed?'

Megsie had to think quickly. 'They've gone out – to – to the field,' she said, and then turned away to blush because she wasn't used to telling fibs.

'Yes,' said Celia, who was, 'they've gone to check the barley.'

'Oh,' said Mrs Green. 'Well, they'll be back soon, won't they?'

'Isabel . . .' said Phil, waggling the fountain pen at her, 'we've got to get on with this!'

'I've got to read it first, haven't I?' said Mrs Green, picking up the contract and studying it closely.

Megsie closed her eyes. What could she do?

The Diary

I'm sorry to interrupt the story as it's getting rather tense but just freeze-frame everyone in your head and then when you get back to it, it'll be even more exciting, I hope.

We're getting ready in a car park near Euston Station.

Oh, the glamour. Today is a very exciting day because we are filming with the Horse Guards! It's a bit of the story that isn't in the book, where Nanny McPhee and the boys get held up by a lot of horses' bottoms. The horses – and their bottoms – belong to the Horse Guards – the special regiment that guards the Queen – and they are so, so beautiful. The Guards are all very young and each one of them has his own horse and has to look after it day and night. They work with the horses every day and live with them all the time – it is a very intense life and they don't really get any time off at all. I was very impressed by them all – these lads who live and breathe their animals and have a very close relationship to each other as well. It must be very hard work, but also very rewarding.

Today is also special because my Stunt Double (see Glossary), Ray De Haan, is on set. He is dressed exactly like me but has to do one thing I can't do – and that is to drive the motorcycle right up to the horses' bottoms and brake hard to avoid running into them. I have had lessons on the bike (I LOVE it) but I am not experienced enough to do this bit without everyone worrying about me actually ramming the bottoms and hurting either the horses or the children. So I will do the close-up motorcycle riding, like when Nanny arrives at the War

Office and leaves and so forth, and Ray will do the expert stuff that takes years of experience.

It is very peculiar having someone on set who looks the same as me. He has the nose and everything.

'It's so HOT and HEAVY,' he said, which was a great comfort to me. I also have another double who stands in for me while they get shots ready and sometimes has to do what we call Second Unit work (see Glossary), stuff like faraway shots that don't need actors to speak or that use animals and would therefore take too much time to shoot with the main cameras. She is called

Abbie James and is a living saint. She came up to me the other day and said she'd been working with the Second Unit on set at Shepperton during the hot weather and had a very hard time.

'I couldn't breathe properly,' she confessed, which was also very comforting to me. It's nice to know that I'm not the only one suffering . . .

I've just found out that a lot of the young guardsmen are just back from stints in Iraq and that some are off soon to Afghanistan. Gives one food for thought. They have done all their stuff wonderfully well – we have taken over a London street and there are lots of people

watching and waving. It's very jolly. The horses get taken off to Regent's Park for a rest and some water and food so you can go and pat them there without getting in the way. Gaia is playing a little evacuee, in a hat and coat from the 1940s that make her look miles younger, for some reason. Clothes do make such a difference.

We decided to go and have a little lunch out with mates who'd come to visit the set, and we walked down the street and into a nice Spanish restaurant and had tapas, which all sounds very nice and normal until I tell you that I was in the FULL Nanny McPhee costume and make-up and no one took a blind bit of notice.

Seriously. People glanced up and looked away as though it were perfectly normal to see a gigantic lady in black with a huge nose and warts walk into their eatery and sit down to order ham. Interesting. Maybe they did notice and felt sorry for me and didn't like to stare. Anyway, it was fun.

The Story

Lord Gray's office was the largest room either of the boys had ever seen, even Cyril, who had visited some very grand houses in his time. Far, far away at the other end they could just make out a figure standing behind a desk. From where they were standing, the figure seemed quite small, but as they started to walk towards it, both the figure and the desk became bigger and bigger and bigger until they stood before them both, quite dwarfed by the desk and in mortal fear of the person standing behind it, who was staring at them with a brow of thunder. In fact, Lord Gray was not a big man. He was quite normal-sized, but he had a very big effect on you. He had piercing blue eyes that

213

seemed to bore a hole in you wherever they looked and loads of medals and stripes everywhere and he stood up so straight that his feet seemed to hover slightly above the floor as he walked. But he wasn't walking now, he was just staring.

'What on earth is the meaning of this, boy?'

The voice was low and oddly gentle and I don't think Norman could have explained why it put such a fear into him. There was something underneath the voice that seemed to say,

'I could eat you very easily at any moment,' as though the man were a bear in disguise or something. Norman looked at Cyril's pale face and thought he understood a bit better what it had cost Cyril to bring him here.

'Sorry to disturb you, sir,' said Cyril, in a voice at least an octave higher than usual. 'We need your help — we . . . we've come all the way up from the country —'

'We?' interrupted Lord Gray, raising a withering eyebrow.

Norman stepped up to stand beside Cyril. 'He means me, Uncle. I mean, Uncle Your Lordship.'

'And you are?' said Lord Gray, skewering Norman with his stare.

'Norman, sir. Norman Green.'

'Enlighten me further, Green,' said Lord Gray.

'Your nephew, sir,' said Norman, uncertainly, as though Lord Gray might not know what a nephew was.

'Aunt Isabel's son,' said Cyril, helpfully.

'Ah, yes,' said Lord Gray. 'The girl who made that unfortunate marriage.'

You remember all that, of course. Lord and Lady Gray had always felt rather embarrassed for Isabel, cut off without a penny and living in squalor amongst the peasants. Norman was so infuriated that he completely lost his fear of Lord Gray and said, quite angrily, 'A happy marriage to my father, sir, who's fighting for your army, so I'll thank you to be more civil!'

Both father and son looked at Norman in amazement – Cyril, because he would never have dared to speak to his father in such a tone, and Lord Gray because no one had in fact spoken to him like that since he was about eight years old. It had an unexpected effect on him – instead of losing his famous temper as Cyril fully expected, he seemed to calm down a bit, coming around the desk to get a closer look at Norman.

'And what is your business here, pray?' he enquired, even more silkily.

'Sir, we need you to find out what's happened to Norman's father. To Uncle Rory,' said Cyril, who, emboldened by Norman, had found a stronger voice. Norman took up the cue.

'He's been away for months and months and he missed his last leave and he hasn't written even though we've sent so many letters, specially

Vinnie, and then yesterday we got a telegram saying – saying that he'd been killed in action – but I know it's wrong! I know he's alive!'

Norman stopped and waited. Lord Gray sucked in his top lip, and seemed to consider for a moment what he had heard.

'I see,' he said finally. 'So you are saying, in effect, that the telegram, a telegram from the War Office itself, contained false information?'

'Exactly!' said Norman.

'And you have proof, of course, otherwise you would not have dared to come here,' said Lord Gray, almost musingly.

Cyril's heart sank. He could tell by his father's tone that he was gearing up for the kill. He also knew that Norman had nothing like what his father would consider proof. Lord Gray continued to speak, his voice becoming milder and milder as he moved closer to the boys.

'Has he contacted you since you received the telegram?'

'No,' said Norman, beginning to realise what was coming.

'Then one of his unit has been in touch, presumably?'

'No,' said Norman, in a much smaller voice.

'Then what proof have you?' said Lord Gray, in a voice so quiet the boys had to lean in to hear him.

Norman knew he had no proof. He knew that Lord Gray was the sort of adult who would never believe him when he said what he was about to say. But he was a brave boy and he was determined so he said it anyway.

'I can feel it in my bones.'

Cyril closed his eyes in despair. Why hadn't they thought of this? Why had he dragged Norman all this way just to be swallowed alive by his father's wrath? Why hadn't he thought it through?

Lord Gray's eyebrows had shot up until they almost joined his hairline.

'Feel it in your bones?' he said, in a loud voice.

'Feel it in your bones?' he said again, in a much louder voice.

Norman gulped.

'Yes,' he whispered, his knees knocking.

Lord Gray's eyebrows knitted together in an almighty frown as he took in a huge breath.

Both the boys quailed. When he spoke it was in a voice so loud that the very walls of the office shook and a small brass figurine of Britannia fell over on the desk.

'Great heavens, boy, you mean to say you've persuaded my weak-willed son to bring you here in the middle of a WAR with some COCK-AND-BULL story about a FEELING you have in your BONES?'

Norman knew then that all was lost. He knew that Lord Gray would never believe him, no matter what he did or said. He was appalled that Lord Gray should describe Cyril in such an awful, untruthful way, and he also knew that he had nothing left to lose. So he just made his voice as big as he could and shouted back:

'He's NOT weak-willed! It was him who saved the piglets and him that thought of helping by coming here, which was very brave! And I know I'm right about my father. Can't you just enquire, PLEASE?'

Once again, the effect was startling. Lord Gray looked so surprised to be shouted at that it was almost comical after his fury. He came very close to Norman, so close that Norman could smell the pipe smoke on his breath.

'There are thousands of men fighting in my army. Why should I give your father, however worthy he may be, my special attention?'

To this, Norman had no answer. He stammered, 'I – I don't know.'

Cyril couldn't bear it. He took his courage in both hands and looked squarely into his father's eyes. 'Because they love him! And so does Auntie Isabel, and they need him! And I know why you sent us away to them too! It had nothing to do with bombs! I know you and Mother are getting a divorce –'

'ENOUGH!' cried Lord Gray.

'NO!' said Cyril. 'You will listen! You've made your lives and our lives a misery! Isn't that enough for you?'

Lord Gray was momentarily unable to speak.

'At least help Uncle Rory and Auntie Isabel to be together,' finished Cyril.

Norman looked at Cyril in awe. He and his father were just staring at each other and panting slightly, like two dogs who've just had a fight.

'Who told you about the divorce, boy?' said

Lord Gray finally, and in a very different voice, a sort of naked voice.

'Nobody told me,' said Cyril miserably. 'They didn't have to.'

'What do you mean?' said Lord Gray.

Cyril thought for a moment, and then, looking utterly wretched, said quietly, 'I could feel it in my bones.'

There was a very loud silence. Norman had that wobbly feeling in his throat that you get just before you start crying. Cyril looked small and defeated but calm too. Lord Gray turned and walked towards a small door behind the giant desk. It was over, thought Norman. They would have to go back without proof, and his mum would sell the farm and one day his dad would come home to find that his life had disappeared.

But Lord Gray turned to them when he reached the door and said, expressionlessly, 'Wait here.'

Back in the kitchen at Deep Valley Farm, Mrs Green was on page three of the contract. Phil was standing over her with his pen at the ready.

'Hurry it up there, Isabel,' he said.

'Mum,' said Megsie, for the umpteenth time, 'please wait for Norman!'

'There's absolutely nothing Norman can do,' said Mrs Green. 'Just stop it, Megsie. It's all difficult enough as it is.'

Phil shot a hard glance at Megsie, who was biting her lip and wondering what on earth she could do to prevent her mother from signing. Suddenly, there was an ear-splitting shriek. It was Celia. She'd got up on to a chair and was screaming, 'A mouse! A mouse!' and pointing over to the cooker. Everyone looked.

'Argh! Aaaarrggh!!! A mouse under the cooker, a big fat mouse, aaaaarghh!!!'

Phil, who was terrified of mice, got nervously on to the settle, while Mrs Green, wincing at the screams, got up and started to poke about under the cooker with a fly-swat. Megsie looked up at Celia who, continuing to scream, pointed urgently at the kitchen table. Megsie looked and saw Phil's fountain pen lying by the contract. Then she understood Celia's plan. Quick as a flash, she picked up the pen and hid it in her tool apron. Neither of the adults saw, engrossed as they were by the mouse drama and deafened as they were by Celia's screeching.

While Celia was giving this fine performance, Norman was pacing up and down in front of Lord Gray's desk until Cyril finally said, 'You'll wear a hole in the carpet if you go on like that.'

'I know,' said Norman apologetically. 'It's just that I can't seem to stop moving.'

He looked at Cyril and saw a very sad expression.

'Are they really going to get divorced, your mum and dad?' he said.

In those days, I should tell you, divorce wasn't quite so common as it is now and people were quite shocked by it when it happened. So Cyril felt awful when he had to say, 'Yes.' It made him feel oddly ashamed, as though it were in some obscure way his fault, which it wasn't.

Norman looked at him compassionately.

'You know, you can come and stay with us. Live with us. You and Celia. Not just wartime. All the time.'

Cyril looked at him and there was a glimmer of light in his eyes.

'Thanks,' he said. 'That's jolly decent of you. Thanks.'

At that moment, the little door opened and Lieutenant Addis came in with a long length of white tape. Lord Gray followed, wearing glasses. Both men looked very grave.

'I'm sorry,' said Lord Gray, consulting the tape.

'What? What does it say?'

'I'm afraid he's M.I.A.'

'What's that?' said Norman, dread in his heart.

Cyril came forward and put a consoling hand on his friend's arm. 'Missing In Action. I'm sorry, Norman.'

Everyone looked very serious. Norman couldn't understand it.

'Wait —' he said. 'Wait — missing in action? Not killed in action, like it said?'

'Not killed,' said Lord Gray. 'The telegram you received was — incorrect. In fact, there's no record of any telegram having been sent —'

Before Lord Gray could finish the sentence, Norman had flung his arms around his neck and was hugging him so tightly he nearly choked. Lieutenant Addis gave another of his little shrieks and dropped the ticker tape.

'I knew it! He's alive!' cried Norman. 'Oh, thank you, Uncle!'

'My nephew,' said Lord Gray to his aide. 'Rough diamond, as they say.'

The rough diamond was already racing down the carpet to the door, shouting for Cyril.

'Come on, we've got to get back! There's no time to lose!'

Cyril looked at his father uncertainly for a

moment and then turned to follow Norman. He'd got halfway down the room when Lord Gray called out, in a very un-military way, 'Cyril, wait!'

Cyril turned and saw his father walking down to meet him. When he'd got close enough, Lord Gray didn't seem to know quite what to do. Then he said, 'Done you good, all that country air.' His voice sounded rough and unsure, almost as though that wasn't what he had wanted to say at all. Cyril just nodded and stood there, feeling foolish. Then Lord Gray held out his hand and said, 'Carry on.'

Cyril shook the proffered hand, feeling very adult and special all of a sudden.

'I will, sir,' he said proudly. 'I mean, I will, Father. Righto.'

'Righto,' said Lord Gray, the right side of his top lip twisting slightly, which might have been the beginnings of a smile but might just as easily have been indigestion.

Cyril decided that the conversation was probably over and joined Norman at the door. Taking a last look at his father, standing looking rather alone in the huge chamber, Cyril gave a small salute and the boys left.

The Diary

We're back at Wormsley and the barley has been harvested! Oh, joy! Lots of wonderful little stacks and a couple of giant ricks that you can climb up on. It looks very beautiful. Monet would have wanted to paint it, I reckon. Lindsay is in the hotel with flu and isn't allowed back to the set until they have decided it isn't swine flu. Oo-er. She's going mad, of course, with frustration, but we will all be OK and just get on with it.

Spent two hours in the make-up caravan having hair prettified for nicer-looking Nanny, only to get out of the car into so much wind and rain that the entire hairdo was destroyed in seconds. Much wailing and gnashing of teeth from Paula.

It is raining heavily. We are up the creek. Everyone deeply depressed. Little tents everywhere, with crew and cast sheltering in the vain hope that the skies may clear and we can shoot something. Each other, possibly.

I have had a day off and it seems to have made matters worse. I am like a dysfunctional clockwork mouse. I keep winding myself up and going off at a fair lick, but then my workings run down so quickly that there must be something wrong somewhere. A spring missing or some such. I no longer have the oomph to write in between takes. I just stare into space or lie down if I can find something to lie on. We've just a month to go and have done about two and a half months so far. Quite a long time to keep all this up, I s'pose. Groan.

The Story

Celia was still screeching as Mrs Green gave up trying to flush out the offending mouse. She shouted, 'Celia! Stop screaming! There is NO MOUSE!'

Celia stopped. 'I saw it,' she said meekly.

'It must have escaped.'

'Come along, Isabel, come along!' said Phil, getting down off the settle rather sheepishly. 'Let's get this thing signed off!'

Sighing, Mrs Green went back to the table and looked at the dotted line Phil was pointing at.

'Give me the pen then,' she said.

Phil looked and looked again.

'What . . . Where the . . . Where's it gone?' he said, patting his pockets anxiously. 'It was just here a second ago –'

'Oh, for heaven's sake, Phil!' said Mrs Green, thoroughly irritated. 'I thought you wanted me to sign the thing!'

'I do! I do! But it's just gone –'

'There're pens on the dresser,' said Mrs Green, and Celia looked with alarm at Megsie. Phil found three pens and put them on the table next to the contract.

Megsie was distraught. She couldn't think of any way of preventing her mother from signing. Then she had a thought. She didn't know quite where it had come from, but it definitely sprang into her head like a cuckoo coming out of its clock. She ran to a quiet corner and stared fiercely up at the ceiling. Then, feeling slightly bonkers, she hissed, 'Nanny McPhee, we need you!'

Nothing happened. Once more, she hissed, 'Nanny McPhee, help! Help! We need you!'

Turning round, she half expected to find Phil had disappeared in a puff of smoke with contract, pens and all, but no, he was still there, leaning over her mother with three perfectly good pens lying there ready to be used.

The kitchen door opened quietly. No one noticed something coming in and getting under the kitchen table.

Norman and Cyril, in the meantime, were rushing down the steps of the War Office at top speed.

Suddenly, Norman stopped and turned to Cyril with a shocked expression. 'Hang on!' he said. 'If the War Office *didn't* send a telegram, then the one we got must have been forged!'

Cyril stared at him. 'But – that's awful,' he said. 'Who would forge a telegram that said someone was dead? Who would do such a terrible thing?'

'I think I know,' said Norman grimly. 'Come on! We've got to hurry!'

Outside, Mr Edelweiss was in the grip of terrible collywobbles and having a strip torn off him by Nanny McPhee.

'Where did you find it this time?' she said, frowning at him.

Mr Edelweiss squawked and burped at length until Nanny McPhee shushed him.

'Now you just listen to me for once,' she said, very sternly. 'You *must* understand that all that comes of eating it is the destruction of other people's property and recurring collywobbles.'

Mr Edelweiss burped sadly.

'I don't care how much you love it,' said Nanny McPhee. 'It is a very nasty habit and we'd all be far better off if you never did it again. Do you hear?'

Mr Edelweiss nodded and let out a final rolling and tremendously resonant burp.

'Oh, don't be so *disgusting*,' said Nanny McPhee, turning away from him crossly. At that very moment both the boys shot out of the great door and came running over, shouting, 'Quickly! Quickly, we've got to get back!'

As they put on their goggles and breathlessly told Nanny McPhee the good news about Mr Green, she started up the engine and, no sooner had their bottoms touched the seat, sped off with a very ill Mr Edelweiss in hot pursuit.

Sergeant Jefferies watched them go.

'Goodbye, Nanny McPhee,' he said to himself rather sadly, as, just along the way, several panes of putty-less glass dropped out of their windows and on to the sandbags below.

In the kitchen, Megsie and Celia were in agonies. Mrs Green was on the last page of the contract and Phil was speeding her through the difficult bits. Megsie clutched Celia's hand, but Celia could only shake her head despairingly. But suddenly, something very odd indeed appeared just at the edge of the table where the pens were lying. One of the pens shot off the table and disappeared. Megsie and Celia looked at each other in absolute astonishment. What on earth was that? They looked – and there it was again! A little grey tube thing with red hairs on it – and SUCK!! Another of the pens disappeared.

It was the baby elephant's trunk!

Megsie had to stuff her hand into her mouth to keep from exploding with hysterical laughter. Celia actually let out a small squeak of excited shock, but luckily Mrs Green and Phil were both ensconced in the contract and didn't see or hear any of it. There was one last pen left. The little trunk came up again, this time further down the table. It sucked and the last pen shot across the table and into the trunk. There was a whiffle of what could have been elephant mirth as the little creature wobbled out of the kitchen door, helped by Vincent, who had seen it all and was doubled up with silent giggles.

Very suddenly, Phil stood up. The girls

whirled back to watch as he laid the contract down in front of Mrs Green and pointed at the dotted line.

'Righto. There it is, simple, really – here we are, and here's a –'

Phil shrieked. There were no pens at all where once there had been three.

'What . . . Where *are* they? They were here!!' he shouted, looking accusingly at Megsie and Celia.

'We didn't touch them!' said Megsie. 'How could we? We were standing here.'

The girls both assumed innocent expressions and stood away from the table, holding up their empty hands for the grown-ups to see. Mrs Green also suspected the girls, but couldn't really see how they had got around to pick up the pens without either Phil or her noticing them moving. She frowned at them warningly and then spoke with unaccustomed harshness to Phil.

'Come along, Phil,' said Mrs Green. 'Get a grip. If you want the thing signed, then find a pen.'

Phil rolled up a sleeve and started to pat the

inside of his elbow. 'Not to worry – we'll sign it in my blood.'

Everyone stared at him as he came round to Megsie.

'I'll just open a vein and then all we need is a quill from one of the chickens and it's done – lend me your penknife there, Megs—'

He put his hand into Megsie's tool apron for the knife, and it came out holding his original fountain pen.

'Oh!' said Phil, giving Megsie a truly evil look. 'Look what I've found!'

Keeping his eye very firmly on the girls, he took Mrs Green's hand and put the pen into it. Then he guided her hand to the line on the paper. Mrs Green sighed heavily and started to write. Megsie let out a sob.

'That's it, Isabel,' said Phil, his voice heavy with relief. 'Isabel Gree—'

THUD!!!

The kitchen shook, and Mrs Green stabbed the pen into the contract, releasing a cloud of ink over the dotted line. Everyone was completely silent for a moment and then started to shout all at once as they ran to the kitchen window to see what on earth the noise had been.

Out of the window, beyond the hedge and in the middle of the barley field stuck a massive green metal tail fin stuck up, like the end of half a rocket.

'What in heaven's name is that?' said Mrs Green, still shaking from the shock.

'It's a UXB!' said Celia.

'What's that?' said Megsie.

'An unexploded bomb. We have them in London quite a lot. It could go off at any second.'

'WHAT?' screeched Vincent, who had rushed back into the kitchen and was standing behind them. Everyone jumped with fright.

'But then again, it might not. Depends,' said Celia, sounding impressively unruffled.

'But they don't drop bombs in the country!' said Megsie. 'It must be a mistake!'

From behind them came a voice barely recognisable as Phil's, it was so hoarse and broken.

'It's not a mistake,' he said. 'It's the sign!'

They all turned to look at him. He was standing with his back against the wall, staring out of a face like a grey mask.

'What are you talking about, Phil?' said Mrs Green, completely mystified.

'They're coming for me!' said Phil, covering his face with his hands.

Mrs Green was just about to enquire further when another voice was heard outside, sounding somewhat amplified as it shouted, 'Stop panicking!! Unexploded bomb is at hand!! Help has landed!!! Stop it!!!!'

In burst Mr Spolding, very pink in the cheeks and yelling through a loudhailer.

Phil rushed to him. 'They're going to kill me!!!' he said.

'Who's going to kill you, Phil?' said Mrs Green.

'Stop all that panicking, I said!!!' shouted Mr Spolding through the loudhailer.

'I can't stop it!' said Phil. 'I'm going to die!'

'I'm going to get under the table,' said Vincent.

'I'm going to put the kettle on,' said Mrs Green, deciding that the only thing for it was for everyone to have a cup of tea and calm down a bit.

'Mine's a milk and two sugars,' yelled Mr Spolding through the loudhailer.

Phil got as close as he could to Mr Spolding. 'Mr Spolding, you have to arrest me! You have to arrest me before they get here because it's the only way I'll be safe! You have to put me in official custody!'

'In what?' said Mr Spolding, looking confused and still speaking through the loudhailer.

Phil grabbed the hailer from him and shouted back at Mr Spolding, 'Arrest me!' Put me in a – what you called it – a fishy custard!'

Mr Spolding now grabbed the hailer and shouted back at Phil, 'Arrest you for what? What for? What've you done? There's got to be a crime!'

From the kitchen door came a voice everyone knew very well. It was Norman's.

'Try forgery!' he said.

The Diary

You can very easily freeze that moment in your heads, can't you? Norman standing there looking very heroic, everyone staring up at him or down at him depending on who they are, and Mrs Green about to pour the tea. There.

Nice day! Nice weather! We are at Tilsey Farm at what we call the carousel field because it was where we shot the piglets flying around the tree (they weren't really flying, of course, it was me and all the children's mums and dads running around holding foam piglets and singing silly songs). There's no loo paper in my trailer, so halfway through this morning I had a rather nasty moment in my corset and curls. That's filming for you. Very little in the way of personal dignity is left by the end of a long shoot. Most people have seen you either cry, lose your temper, vomit, hit things for no reason, whinge – or in this case, seen your bottom, which is really the lowest point in my view. Rather unpleasant altogether, but there it is.

Our fabulous Mr Green is on set to do a flashback scene (he's a bit of a secret so I'm saying nothing here about who it is) and being as gorgeous and funny and loving and great as Mr Green could ever be. All the females on set are trembling slightly. Bit like releasing a particularly genetically suitable bull into a herd of slightly somnolent cows. We've all woken up a bit and are milling about, mooing at each other and preening.

August 1st: We've all just had two days off and are feeling rather chipper! Ralph Fiennes is in giving his Lord Gray (we sometimes say 'give' instead of 'play' – I don't know why, it's an acting term, I suppose). He is wonderful. Chilling and full of internal pains and conflict and buried emotions. He and I spent lunchtime discussing Pasolini's film *Salo*, which seemed to be all about poo. I feel rather ill now. It might also be because the family left for hols in Scotland this morning and I am alone in the house with Oatcake the hamster.

Went to set glumly and was greatly cheered by Ed Stoppard (Lieutenant Addis) and Ralph and the boys (Asa and Eros) being brilliant in the scene. Rhys is back, his foot all better – hurrah! When I first saw him in his wig and costume I didn't actually recognise him. Peter King and Jackie Durran deserve medals for that creation.

August 4th: Weather out here is so bad that we've moved the entire unit back to Shepperton. Ghastly business – everyone has to pack up their gear, tons and tons of it, and load it on to lorries and trucks and then drive and unload it and set it all up again, crossly, and then have half an hour to shoot what we needed the whole day for. It's no fun and it makes everyone incredibly grumpy. I feel that I may be shooting this film for

Emma's in the way!

the rest of my life, and I'm not the only one. Susanna had to wave her girls off the other day too. I've told her she can borrow Oatcake if she gets too lonely. He's quite a laugh, if you like that sort of thing. Filming is even worse for directors because they have to be there before everything starts and after everything stops FOR AGES, sorting out the day or watching the stuff we've shot. It is a brutal schedule.

August 6th: Oh dear. Was mucking about on the picnic set, trying to make the children laugh, saw a cricket bat and, thinking it was the rubber one that Vinnie uses in the first bit of the story, proceeded to hit myself very hard in the face with it. It wasn't the rubber one and I now have a very sore face. Mind you, they laughed. Luckily I didn't bruise, so even though I complained like anything, as soon as they realised nothing was going to show, everyone lost interest and ignored me.

August 8th: Doing all Phil's scenes with Topsey and Turvey, which is complete fun. We're filming outside on the Getty estate, which is so beautiful and peaceful. Went home, talked to Oatcake, watched two French films, picked up fallen damsons and collected cucumbers from the greenhouse. Nice things to do.

August 10th: You see, what no one *tells* you about jackdaws is that they *smell*.

I think it's all the raw meat they eat. All the birds have been fantastic. I started training with them in February (they live at Leavesden, which is where all the Harry Potters are filmed) and, like I said, they remember everything. Such clever creatures. They're not like pets or anything, you can't stroke them, but you can talk to them and they will talk back, and once they get on to my shoulder, they'll stay there for ages, just chatting away. I'm very fond of them all, but particularly the youngest whose name is Al. He has a most endearing personality and a cheeky look in his eye.

We're shooting somewhere called Hambledon soon. Apparently someone called Lady Hambledon wants to say hello to me – she must own the place . . .

Bill Bailey is back today with a horse and wagon. The horse is huge and doesn't look like a horse at all. Bill says it is not, in fact, a horse but a giant bulldog in a horse costume. There were fireworks outside my hotel window last night so didn't get to sleep until late. I am so tired today that I lay down at lunch and didn't move a muscle for an hour and a half. Apparently there are only fourteen more shooting days. Can't be true. We are nearly finished. But all the stuff we have yet to

shoot is HUGE so it's not just a matter of mopping up little bits here and there. Martin, our First AD, will leave next week – a holiday that can't be cancelled. Several folk are dropping away as we go on into the summer, because no one foresaw we would shoot for quite this long. Even I will have to leave two days before the bitter end, which feels most odd and like some awful betrayal of everyone.

August 12th, I think: We're shooting the picnic scene so, of course, it's raining. The Art Department have finally got the cowpat right. I wrote this sentence in the script: Mrs Docherty spies a big cowpat.

'Oh look!' she says. 'How thoughtful! You've put out cushions!'

I didn't describe the cowpat in any great detail, but I saw in my head one of those round things with a dip in the middle that really could be mistaken for a brown cushion if you couldn't see very well and were slightly bonkers, both of which apply to Mrs Docherty. But the first cowpat that arrived was – well, it was terribly realistic, of course, because we have a brilliant Art Department, who went and looked at lots of real cowpats and produced an exact replica. Anyway, it was green, with bits of stuff sticking out here and there, and Maggie Smith took one look at it and said, 'You must be joking! I wouldn't sit on that – it looks like a pile of sick.' We all laughed heartily of course, except the Art Department, who had to go away and make a new one. Susanna is going to take pictures of her cowpats at home (she lives on a dairy farm) to make sure that we are getting it right. This new one is perfect and looks as though it would be very comfy if you sat on it.

The cowpat's all right, but Simon (our sound

maestro) has brought in his brand-new sound machine with sixteen tracks on it because there are ten people in this scene – and it's broken. We are DOOMED.

The Story

Everyone whirled around to see Norman standing in the doorway looking very stern and pointing an accusing finger at Phil. Flanking him were Cyril and Nanny McPhee looking equally grave.

'Norman!' cried Mrs Green. 'Where on earth have you been?'

This was Norman's big moment – he'd thought about it from the moment the awful telegram had arrived and he'd known it was false and he'd wanted to shout it then but knew he couldn't, but now he had proof and he could. He took a deep breath.

'Mum – Dad's alive.'

Vincent breathed in sharply. 'What?' he said, in a tiny squeaky voice.

'Dad's alive and I can prove it.'

Mrs Green sat down very suddenly. Luckily there was a chair behind her so she didn't fall on the floor.

'How?' she said, very quietly.

Norman walked over to her. 'Cyril and I went to the War Office in London with Nanny

McPhee. We saw Cyril's dad and found out that Dad was M.I.A.'

'That means Missing In Action,' said Cyril helpfully.

'And we found out something else – no telegram was ever sent – the one we got was forged!'

'Exactly!' cried Phil with relief. 'And I forged it! I'm an evil forger! There's your crime! Now will you arrest me?'

But Mr Spolding was gazing with admiration at Norman and Mrs Green, who had tears in her eyes that made them shine even brighter.

'Norman – how did you know Dad was still alive?' she asked.

'I could feel it in my bones,' said Norman, without hesitation.

Mrs Green looked at him for a long moment.

'Then it must be true,' she said, getting up and hugging him to her chest. 'Thank you, my darling, thank you, thank you.'

And then some of the tears fell on top of Norman's head but he didn't notice them.

'And Cyril! Thank Cyril too!' he said, somewhat indistinctly.

Mrs Green cried, 'Oh, Cyril darling, come here!'

And he did, and Mrs Green hugged him to the other side and nearly suffocated them both, and Mr Spolding wept a small tear as well, because he was so happy to hear that lovely Rory Green was alive.

'Didn't you hear?' shrieked Phil, clutching at Mr Spolding's arm. 'I'm a forger, a villainous forger! Arrest me, please, before it's too late!!!'

But Mr Spolding had started to consult his pamphlet.

'Leave it, Phil,' he said, crossly. 'There's a bomb out there what needs dealing with.'

This was the first the boys had heard of it. Everyone went to the window again.

'It's a UXB!' said Cyril.

'They know,' said Celia. 'I just told them.'

'It could go off at –'

'They know that too,' said Celia, patiently. 'We've been through all that. The question is – what do we do now?'

'Don't we run away?' said Vincent, looking concerned.

'No!' said Norman. 'It's right in the middle of

the barley! If it goes off, the whole harvest will be destroyed! Mr Spolding! What does it say in the book?'

Mr Spolding held up a finger and read out the following:

'"Defusing your bomb. Four Simple Steps to an Explosion-Free day."'

'Can't you at least cuff me?' said Phil, despairingly. 'So as they see I'm under arrest? They won't be able to touch a person who's in custard and cuffs!'

'Here, Phil, do it yourself,' said Mr Spolding, throwing him a pair of handcuffs. 'I've got work to do.' And with that he walked out of the door towards the bomb.

'Shouldn't we help him?' said Norman worriedly.

'Certainly not!' said Mrs Green. 'He's a fully fledgling professional, leave it to him.'

'Megsie, help me with these, will you?' said Phil, helplessly trying to cuff himself up.

Now that Mr Spolding was dealing with the bomb, everyone had time to remember what a terrible thing Phil had done. They all turned and stared at him. He quailed.

'You don't deserve any help, you completely *wicked* person!' said Megsie.

'Please!' said Phil. 'I'm begging you!'

'Allow me,' said Mrs Green, in an icy voice that none of her children had ever heard before. She went over, led Phil to the oven range and cuffed him to the iron bar above, where the saucepans hung.

'Thank you, Isabel,' said Phil, in pathetic tones.

Just then, Mr Spolding's voice was heard through the loudhailer and everyone turned away from Phil and back to the window.

Mr Spolding had put a ladder up against the

side of the bomb and was on top of it, shouting towards the house. 'I am about to disarm the device,' he intoned. 'If I succeed there will be no further peril or untimely demise –'

He lowered the loudhailer for a moment, but lifted it again as though struck by a new thought.

'And if I don't succeed,' he shouted, sounding a little less confident, 'there will be lots of peril and we'll all die, especially me, cos I'm closest.'

Then he lowered the hailer again and lifted the pamphlet, wobbled slightly, wobbled a bit more, gave a tiny moan and fell backwards off the ladder and into the barley. There was a dead silence.

'He fell over,' said Vincent, in case no one else had noticed.

'I think he may have fainted,' said Mrs Green.

'That's useful,' said Cyril.

'Who's going to defuse it now?' said Norman.

'I bet Megsie could!' said Celia.

'Oh, don't be ridiculous!' said Mrs Green, but found herself shouted down by five children all crying, 'Yes! Yes! Megsie can do it! Let her try!'

Mrs Green was adamant, but finally Norman

caught her arm and said, 'Mum – listen, if that thing goes off, the crop will be destroyed and it will all have been for nothing!'

'Oh, please let me try!' begged Megsie.

'There's an official pamphlet!' said Cyril. 'What could go wrong?'

All the children started to march off in a determined pack.

'All of you, come *back* here, right now!' shouted Mrs Green, following them.

'Help me to stop them, Nanny McPhee!' she cried as she ran out of the door.

'I doubt that will be possible,' said Nanny McPhee, allowing herself just the slightest hint of a smile before she too left the kitchen.

Phil was left alone. He examined the bar he was cuffed to. It was good and strong. Even if the hit-women came, they wouldn't be able to take him away, he reckoned. He was as safe here as anywhere and a lot safer than the rest of the family, who were probably going to get blown up. Which meant that the farm would be available after all. He brightened slightly. Things were looking up.

In the field, Mrs Green had failed to stop the

children from taking action and had gone with them to see if Mr Spolding was all right after his fall. While she and Vincent fanned him, Megsie issued orders:

'Boys, put that ladder back up! Celia, you've got the best diction and the loudest voice, you read out the instructions.'

Megsie shimmied up the ladder like a monkey and called out, 'Right, I'm in position. Go!'

'Step One,' said Celia, in her clearest tones. 'Open the vent situated by the tail fin with a screwdriver.'

Megsie looked at the bomb – there was the vent, right in front of her. She whipped out a screwdriver and tried it but it was too small, so she got the next size up, which fitted perfectly. Taking a deep breath, she attacked the screws, extracting each one quickly and efficiently.

'I'm taking the vent off NOW!' she called out to the others, who were all at the base of the ladder watching her with tense anxiety.

Megsie pulled hard, and with a screech of metal that made her wince she pulled off the vent and flung it away from her into the barley, where it landed with a quiet thud.

'Vent's off!' cried Megsie. 'What's next!'

'Step Two,' said Celia. 'Cut the blue wire.'

Megsie looked into the bomb's innards. She'd been quite calm until now, but the sight that met her eyes gave her a real shock. The bomb was a mess of cables and wires and nuts and bolts that looked as though someone had just pushed them all in without caring where anything went.

'No wonder the blinking thing doesn't work,' she muttered to herself, gingerly using the screwdriver to push aside the mess and find the blue wire. Talking to herself calmed her down slightly and then she saw the wire she wanted nestling next to some others which were different colours. She took out a pair of wire-cutters from her tool apron. At the bottom of the ladder, Norman was panting with tension.

'Have you done it?' he said.

'No! These are too small!' cried Megsie, waving the cutters at the others. 'Has anyone got a penknife or something?'

Everyone searched their pockets frantically until Celia gave a shout. 'Here!' She handed up a pair of nail scissors she'd found in her nail kit.

'Try these!'

'Perfect!' said Megsie gratefully.

With great care, she reached into the bomb again and *SNIP*, cut the blue wire.

'Done!' she announced.

Everyone heaved a sigh of relief. Nothing bad had happened. Everything was going according to plan.

'Step Three!' said Celia. 'Cut the *red* wire.'

Megsie searched for the red wire and finally saw it – deeper down than the blue; she was going to have to reach her body further over the lip of the bomb than felt quite safe. But she was a brave and determined person, so she pulled herself up and stretched inwards.

'It's like being a lion-tamer,' she said to herself. 'I'm putting my head into the lion's mouth.'

Below her, things were getting even tenser.

'What's taking so long?' shouted Norman.

'Can you see it?' shouted Celia.

'Have you done it?' shouted Cyril.

But Megsie was so far inside the bomb she couldn't hear them. All they could see were her legs waving in the air. Mrs Green was biting her fist to keep herself from screaming. She was desperate to get everyone away but she knew that they couldn't move Mr Spolding, who was still out cold, and she couldn't think of any way she could move the children, except by carrying them bodily away one by one, which would never work. The suspense rose. Everyone stopped breathing.

'Isn't it EXCITING!!!' said a very loud voice. They all jumped ten feet in the air and whirled round to find Mrs Docherty standing there, gazing at the bomb with huge enthusiasm.

'Shh!' they all said. 'Megsie's trying to defuse it!'

'Ooooh!' said Mrs Docherty, thrilled, and going to stand beside Mrs Green and Mr Spolding.

'Hello, Algernon,' she said. 'You're not dead, are you?'

Mrs Green whispered an explanation as Megsie's head finally re-emerged from the bomb and she waved the scissors aloft and cried, 'Done! What's Step Four?'

Then, very suddenly, the bomb gave a lurch. Megsie shrieked with alarm.

'Is that supposed to happen?' quavered Mrs

Green, running to look over Celia's shoulder at the pamphlet.

Unseen by all, a little red light on the side of the bomb started to flash. It was in a row of ten . . .

Back in the kitchen, Phil had tried, unsuccessfully, to get comfortable and was now in a very bad mood. He closed his eyes and tried to doze off, but then heard the kitchen door opening.

'At last!' he said grumpily. 'Could someone take these things off –'

He looked over, and there were Miss Topsey and Miss Turvey, both attired in very smart nurses' uniforms and pushing a cloth-covered trolley before them.

'Oo-oo!' they sang, as all the blood drained from Phil's face into his toes.

'We thought we'd bring the sign ourselves!' said Miss Topsey, pushing the trolley up towards Phil.

'But – I thought that was the sign! The bomb!' said Phil, his eyes bulging.

'That?' said Miss Turvey. 'Oh no. That's just a silly old UXB. That needn't concern you Phil, no.'

'You can't do anything to me!' Phil yelled. 'I'm in a fishy custard and cuffs!'

'That's useful,' said Miss Topsey.

'We won't have to tie you down,' said Miss Turvey. 'We've got such good news for you, Phil!'

'We're not going to squash you with farm machinery after all!'

Phil experienced a moment's wild relief. He sagged against the cooker and then stood up again sharpish because it was hot.

'Oh?' he said weakly. 'That's – that's good. Why's that, then?'

'Because Mrs Big decided squashing wasn't good enough for you,' said Miss Topsey.

'It lacked finesse,' said Miss Turvey.

'Too messy,' explained Miss Topsey, in case Phil didn't know what finesse meant, which he didn't.

'So – what she wants is . . .' said Miss Turvey, looking terribly excited.

'She wants us to . . .' said Miss Topsey, looking equally thrilled.

'She wants us to STUFF YOU!!!' they chorused joyfully.

Phil blinked. He couldn't quite take it in. 'What?' he said.

'She wants us to stuff you and put you in the entrance to the London casino! As a warning to others!' cried Miss Topsey.

'What an honour, Phil!' breathed Miss Turvey, looking at Phil as though she quite envied him.

Phil thought he was going to be sick. 'You can't do that!' he said, knowing full well that they could and would.

'Oh, don't you worry, Phil,' said Miss Topsey.

'Miss Turvey's a professional!'

Here, Miss Turvey looked down bashfully and opened her handbag. 'Here's an early example of my work,' she said shyly, pulling out a large owl, expertly stuffed and mounted on a shiny brass pedestal.

Miss Topsey opened her bag and pulled something else out. 'And here's how you'll look!' she said, putting a model figure, also mounted on a brass pedestal, next to the owl. The figure looked exactly like Phil, down to the stripes on his tie and the look of terror on his face.

Both ladies then flung aside the cloth on the trolley to reveal an array of extremely upsetting

surgical instruments, which glinted up at Phil
evilly. Miss Topsey picked up the oddest of
them. It was a large ladle, such as you might use
for serving soup.

'The only trouble is, Phil . . .' said Miss Topsey,
'we're going to have to scoop you out while
you're still . . . well . . .'

'Alive,' finished Miss Turvey.

They both looked at Phil apologetically.

'Otherwise you'll go all blotchy,' said Miss
Topsey.

'Which would result in amateurish work,'
shivered Miss Turvey. 'And we don't want that.'

Phil started to scream.

★

Everyone in the field felt like screaming too, but for entirely different reasons. They were all leafing madly through the pamphlet trying to find out why the bomb was moving. No one saw the second red light come on and start to flash next to the first. Megsie was holding on to the ladder for dear life and shouting, 'What does it say? What does it say?!'

Norman yelled up, 'It just says: "Cut the Green Wire."'

'I can't see any green wire!' shrieked Megsie, who'd looked and looked and couldn't see anything green at all. 'It must be covered with all this grey stuff!!'

The bomb started to make a whining noise.

'Uh-oh,' said Vincent.

'Wake up, Algernon, wake up!' shouted Mrs Docherty, slapping Mr Spolding repeatedly around his chops: 'I don't want you to miss it going off!'

Cyril suddenly found something.

'Here it is!' he shouted. '"Warning – if the Green Wire is protected with grey explosive putty, RED LIGHTS will flash and the bomb will now reactivate"! But there aren't any red – oh.'

Cyril had caught sight of the red lights flashing on the side of the bomb. Everyone else looked at them too. 'Why is that at the *back*?' said Cyril, smacking the pamphlet irritably.

As she spoke, the fifth red light came on and started to flash. 'Ooooh,' said Mrs Docherty again. 'Aren't they pretty?'

Mr Spolding was coming round.

'I want everyone to come with me RIGHT NOW,' said Mrs Green commandingly.

'But Mum – the barley –'

'I said NOW,' said Mrs Green.

Celia, Cyril, Norman, Vincent and Mrs Green helped Mr Spolding up and started to limp off with him. At the same time, Mr Edelweiss flapped down on to the lip of the bomb and squawked at Megsie. She looked up at him, a light in her eyes.

'Megsie, get down from there NOW!!!' shouted Mrs Green, leaving the others to find a safe place and running to the foot of the ladder.

'Wait! Wait!!' shrieked Megsie. 'Mr Edelweiss is eating the putty!!'

And so he was.

CHOMP CHOMP CHOMP CHOMP.

All those years of practice had really paid off. You never saw a bird eat such a quantity of putty in no time at all.

'Get DOWN!!' screamed Mrs Green, grabbing at Megsie's legs as the ninth light came on and the whine got so loud she thought her ears would burst. But Megsie could see the shimmer of green appearing as the last of the putty went down Mr Edelweiss's throat.

'MEGSIE!!!' howled Mrs Green, as Megsie kicked her legs free, hurled herself bodily into the bomb and snipped the green wire just before the last light came on. The terrible whine suddenly stopped. There was a little whimper as the bomb ceased to shudder and shake. All the lights went out. An extraordinary peace descended, into which a robin sang a single perfect note.

Below them, Nanny McPhee watched quietly.

'Lesson Four – to be brave – is complete,' she whispered.

Hardly daring to believe what they'd accomplished, Megsie and Mr Edelweiss looked at each other.

Megsie's eyes widened. 'Look,' she breathed.

Mr Edelweiss was enormous. He was huge. He was the size of a space hopper, except they didn't have them in those days. He was the size of a beanbag chair, except they didn't have them either. Put it this way, he was ...

BIG

Nanny McPhee stepped up to the ladder. She looked up at Mr Edelweiss and said, very quietly, 'Silly bird. You're full of explosive putty. You'll go off pop if we're not careful. Get down, Megsie. Go and tell everyone to take cover.'

Staring with wonder at poor Mr Edelweiss, who was looking none too comfortable and not a little concerned, Megsie shimmied down the ladder and went to join the others behind the little abandoned shepherd's hut at the side of the field. After everyone had hugged Megsie and kissed her and thanked her for saving everyone and everything, they all peered out to watch. Nanny McPhee was standing next to the bomb with her arms outstretched. Mr Edelweiss, who couldn't really fly, sort of floated through the air towards her, pathetically trying to flap his wings. She caught him in her hands, very, very gently. Everyone put their fingers in their ears.

Nanny McPhee turned towards the barley and seemed to look up at Mr Edelweiss, with a smile. Then she just let him go. He hovered in the air for a few moments and then . . . he burped. And burped. And burped. On and on and on it went until they saw the heads of the barley begin to bend beneath the wind of the burp, bend and swirl and dance. The wind grew. It grew wilder and wilder, until the children and Mr Spolding and Mrs Docherty and Mrs

Green could no longer keep their eyes open and had to hold on to each other in order not to get blown away.

In the kitchen, Miss Topsey and Miss Turvey had just finished drawing pretty scarlet incision lines across Phil's abdomen when the kitchen windows suddenly blew right open. Phil, who had his eyes closed tight, snapped them open to see Miss Topsey and Miss Turvey being buffeted about by the wind, which was now in the kitchen and blowing a gale. The two women held tight to the table, trying to keep upright. The wind got stronger still and suddenly Phil felt his feet lift slightly off the floor. He gave a shout of alarm until he realised that the women were also being lifted off their feet – but WITHOUT BEING CUFFED TO ANY-THING!!! As the wind lifted him higher, until he was at a right angle to the stove, the cuffs held him safe while the two women, with terrible wails of rage and fright, were bowled off their feet. Miss Topsey cartwheeled neatly out of the door, and Miss Turvey was blown up into the open window, sticking there for a moment before, with a great sucking sound, she was pulled through and away, over the horizon.

Phil was hurled about in the air, screaming for joy, until a very large saucepan fell off the shelves and hit him on the head.

In the field, Norman tried to open one eye to see what was happening but all he caught a glimpse of was a great whirling in the sky, like looking at the sun through a kaleidoscope. On and on it blew, until suddenly the burp-wind stopped and another silence descended. One by one, the children opened their eyes. Vincent saw it first.

'Look!' he cried.

Then Mrs Green saw.

'Oh!' she gasped.

Then Norman saw. He couldn't speak. He just made a noise that was a mixture of aston-ishment and delight.

Then Megsie and Celia saw.

'Look!' they said.

And Mrs Docherty saw.

'The harvest's in!' she said wonderingly.

And so it was.

That great wind had lifted all the stalks of

barley from the field and winnowed them, releasing them back down to the earth in perfectly formed stacks with two huge ricks in the centre. There, in the middle, stood Nanny McPhee, Mr Edelweiss by her side, now quite normal-sized and with a shell-shocked expression on his face. The bomb had completely disappeared.

Slowly at first, everyone came out from behind the hut. Vincent spied the ladder leaning against one of the big ricks.

'Let's climb up!' he shouted joyfully, running towards it. All the other children ran after him, yelling and shouting at the tops of their voices and happier than they had ever been, ever in their lives.

'Three cheers for Mr Edelweiss!!' shouted Mrs Green, and everyone cheered their heads off as Mr Edelweiss gave a very dignified bow. Then he looked at Nanny McPhee furtively and she gave him a big smile and nodded her head as though she was pleased with him. He blinked with pleasure and gave a single proud squawk before joining the children on top of the barley-rick.

The Diary

We are in the beautiful little village of Hambledon, made even more beautiful by the Art Department, who have moved all the cars and put grass everywhere and planted things and made a shop-front for Mrs Docherty's and, oh, it's gorgeous. Lady Hambledon, a delightful Italian person with lilac hair, came out and introduced herself and invited me for pasta at her house. I can't wait. It'll be the first square meal I've had in weeks ...

Maggie, Rhys and Sam are doing the first Mr Spolding scene and all being very funny and terrific.

August 16th: Back at Shepperton. Got all dressed up to try for the final shot of the film, where Nanny lets Mr E. get on her shoulder, and of course it was lovely and sunny in the car park when I arrived, and as soon as I got out of the make-up chair to shoot the scene the sun went behind a cloud and declined to come out again. So I took all the make-up off and Read In (see Glossary) for other people as we picked up a few things in the studio. Then at about 5 p.m. I got into all the make-up again and we went and tried to shoot it for the fifteenth time and the sun went in AGAIN and we all swore at the sky like anything and I took all my make-up off again and went home feeling rather daft.

But I do feel now that this shoot will end. It actually will.

It's when things like this shoot end that you realise life itself *will* one day end too. It somehow makes that more real.

August 17th: Bright, hot, cloudless day. We're inside. Enough to make you weep, it is. Feel utterly depressed by weather and my general ancientness.

August 18th: Heatwave all week. The Law of Sod holds evil sway over us all. We are shooting inside and can't change it around because of people's schedules (mine, mostly, it has to be admitted). Still feel ancient and depressed.

August 19th: Better today. My husband and daughter came to cheer us on. It's even HOTTER in the studio, but we are shooting at a tremendous lick and getting fabulous stuff from everyone. Maggie made me cry every time she delivered the line 'Then it must be true' when Asa tells her Mr Green is still alive. Lots of Kleenex being used around the monitors. Five days to go. I can't believe it.

August 20th: Maggie Gyllenhaal's last day! 40°C in the studio, but everyone on fine form. We all had cupcakes and champagne on wrap! (see Glossary).

Earlier in the day, I passed Oscar's caravan and saw a notice outside that said: DO NOT ENTER. SICK BAY.

Gaia came out and said to me, very urgently, that they'd had to send for Rachel the nurse because Oscar (Vincent) had just fallen down the steps of his caravan and hurt his head. Oh no! I thought, envisaging wounds and horror and going gently in to see what was up. The caravan was full of very quiet people all sitting around Oscar, who had a makeshift bandage round his head and an expression of deep gloom on his face. I was appalled. I went and sat with him. He was silent.

'He can't speak,' said Lil (Megsie). 'He's in shock.'

'We've called an ambulance,' said his mum, Lizzie.

'Oh, Oscar, darling,' I said, tears coming into my eyes. 'Don't worry, we'll get you out of here in no time.'

Guiltily I thought, Help! If Oscar's injured we won't be able to finish this week and then it will be even later and we will all miss our holidays and the studio will be so cross and Eric will fire us and –

And then I heard a tiny, stifled giggle. It was Rosie (Celia), who had caught Gaia's eye. And then I thought, Hang on . . .

And I looked at Oscar's bandage and it did seem to have red crayon on it, as though someone had drawn something to look like blood, and now I came to think of it, he did look quite healthy and Lizzie did seem too calm for a mother with a badly injured son and then I realised.

It was an elaborate and brilliantly executed trick! I had fallen for it hook, line and sinker. I'd even felt quite faint. I nearly bit everyone's ankles to punish them and ran back to the studio with my tail between my legs. I really am the most gullible person on the planet and now they all KNOW, and so do you, for that matter . . .

Got into the full Nanny make-up and then wasn't used at all. Lil and Rosie did a lovely song for Maggie at the end of the day and Lil wept! It was all very moving and we sent Maggie off with huge cheers and tight hugs, all so grateful for her incredibly hard work and wonderful performance. It will feel very strange without our Mrs Green . . .

The Story

Up on the barley-rick, the children were having the time of their lives, sliding down it and then going up the ladder and sliding down again. Everyone had a go, even Mr Spolding, who enjoyed it more than anyone, I think. Mrs Green watched the gaiety with a deep sense of joy that not even the absence of Mr Green could quell. *How proud he'll be*, she kept thinking and every time she had the thought, she smiled and smiled.

Megsie was helping Celia up the ladder for the eighty-fifth time when she noticed something pinned on to the front of Celia's blouse (well it was Megsie's blouse, if you recall, but they both thought of it as Celia's now). It was one of Nanny McPhee's medals.

'Oh!' said Celia, with great surprise. Then, looking up, she saw that Megsie had one too.

'What's that one? I think mine's the one for Kindness!'

'This is Resolve,' said Megsie wonderingly.

They shouted at the others and sure enough, Norman had the medal for Imagination, Cyril the one for Bravery, Vincent the one for Enthusiasm and Mrs Green the one for Leaps of Faith.

'Where's Basketwork?' said Megsie, with interest.

'There!' said Mrs Green, pointing to Mr Edelweiss. On his feathery chest lay the last medal. He hopped up and down with excitement and pride.

'Can he do basketwork?' whispered Celia to Megsie, rather discreetly in case Mr Edelweiss heard and thought she didn't think he deserved a medal.

'I don't know,' said Megsie. 'Maybe she wants him to take it up? She's always said he needs a hobby.'

'That must be it,' said Celia.

'Why has she given us her medals?' said Vincent.

'Let's ask her!' said Celia.

They all looked about, but Nanny McPhee was nowhere to be seen.

'Nanny McPhee!' they all called out. 'Nanny McPhee!'

Celia was on top of the rick and suddenly caught sight of a little black figure right at the edge of the field.

'There she is!' she cried.

'Where's she going?'

Then a gentle voice came from behind the rick. Mrs Docherty appeared, shading her eyes with her hand. She'd been watching Nanny McPhee for some time.

'She's leaving you,' she said.

'WHAT?' said Cyril.

'Why?' said Megsie.

'Because you don't need her any more,' she said.

'Oh, don't be ridiculous!' said Mrs Green.

'Oh dear,' said Mrs Docherty, dropping her arm and looking at the children with a rather sad expression. 'You've forgotten how she works, haven't you?'

Something dim and distant stirred in the

children's memories. Something about wanting and needing but they couldn't remember! All they could recall was how horrible they'd been then, to her and to each other, which made them feel like hugging each other and Nanny McPhee and saying they were sorry all over again.

'How? How does she work?' said Celia worriedly.

Mrs Docherty looked at them all with enormous understanding. 'When you need her but do not want her, then she must stay. When you want her but no longer need her, then she has to go.'

The children and Mrs Green stared at Mrs Docherty, aghast.

'That's not fair!' said Norman.

'We didn't mean to want her!' cried Vincent.

'What do you *mean*, we don't need her?' said Mrs Green, looking at Mrs Docherty as if she were quite mad.

'Come on!' yelled Cyril. 'Let's head her off! We can explain! We can persuade her to stay!!'

Mrs Green led the charge as they all jumped off the barley-rick and ran into the field after the little black figure.

Mrs Docherty watched them, smilingly. 'Oh, Nanny McPhee doesn't like goodbyes,' she said to Mr Spolding. 'I remember from when *I* was little.'

Mr Spolding and Mrs Docherty smiled at each other and sat down to look at the beautiful view together.

The Diary

Last day for Rhys today, and for Katy (Brand, playing Miss Turvey) and Sinead (Matthews, playing Miss Topsey). We're having great fun in the kitchen with stuffed owls and ladles. The wind machine is in as well!

My trailer is stuffed full of farewell gifts to hand out. I feel weirder and weirder. It's the wrap party tomorrow night. Good grief! Our beloved Runner, Darren, is leaving us today. We are all feeling bereft. He's the best Runner I've ever come across. Can't bear to lose him.

Later: Fantastic stuff today! We just did the final shot of Rhys flying in the wind, attached to the iron bar in the kitchen, and it looked amazing. Katy and Sinead are also without peer as Topsey and Turvey. I've had a heavenly day watching these very clever actors being so witty and inventive. Like a major Christmas present you've always wanted and it turns out to be the right size and colour and everything.

The Story

Mrs Green, who had longer legs than the children, was quite far ahead, but no matter how fast she made her legs go she simply couldn't catch up with Nanny McPhee. It was very peculiar because Nanny McPhee looked as if she was going quite slowly, gliding, really, up the lane, and by rights Mrs Green should have reached her a long time ago.

'*They* might not need you,' panted Mrs Green, as loudly as she could without passing out, 'but *I* do! I need you desperately!! Come back!!!'

Behind her, the children, legs aching with the effort but all determined to bring back Nanny McPhee, started to catch up. Nanny McPhee turned the corner. Mrs Green made a huge effort and sprinted the last few yards to follow her round. The children ran as fast as they could, all yelling, 'Keep up, Mum! . . . Keep up, Aunt Isabel!!'

As they too finally rounded the corner, they practically ran into Mrs Green's back. She'd stopped and was staring up the hill with her hand shielding her eyes.

'Come on, Mum, else we'll lose her!' said Norman, pulling at her sleeve.

'Mum, come on, we need her!' said Vinnie.

'No, we don't,' said Mrs Green, still looking and looking.

All the children turned to follow her gaze. At the top of the hill, they could see Nanny

McPhee sharply silhouetted against the bright sky, so sharply they could even see the feathers in her hat dancing in the breeze. She was bowing to someone – it was difficult to see, the light was so bright up there. A man. A man with – what was it? His arm was in a sling. As he turned from Nanny McPhee towards them, they could see the white of the bandage quite clearly. Then their eyes got used to the sun and they saw the colour of his clothes. Khaki. A uniform.

'DAD!!' shouted Vincent.

The man looked up. His good arm shot into the air and a great cry of happiness burst out of him. The children ran and ran, shouting and cheering until they all met in a tumble of arms and legs and hugs and kisses in the grass. Cyril and Celia were close behind and they were hugged and kissed too. Mrs Green was the last to reach them all. That was the biggest hug and kiss of them all.

At the very top of the hill, unnoticed, stood Nanny McPhee.

She watched the scene and smiled the smiliest smile you could ever wish to see.

'Lesson Five – to have faith – is complete,' she said.

There was a small, discreet cough from a nearby branch. Nanny McPhee turned to see Mr Edelweiss looking at her. If he'd had eyebrows, one of them would have been raised at her.

Nanny McPhee thought for a moment. 'I see your point,' she said finally.

Mr Edelweiss let out a squawk of joy.

'Hop on, then,' said Nanny McPhee, patting her shoulder, and on Mr Edelweiss hopped.

If one was to take a bet on who ends up happiest in this story, I'll let you in on a secret. My money's on the jackdaw.

THE END

The Diary

Last day. Argh! So exhausted I can barely manage to finish a sentence. Have got through THREE noses today, the really big ones. The first one melted, the second one just wouldn't stay on no matter what Paula did. Peter King came in and suggested stapling it. We threw him out. Then all the children came in and sang me a song to say goodbye. I cried, of course, and that did it for the last nose. We put it into the bowl that Paula keeps in the fridge, which is full of old noses and looks like the ingredients for some sort of repellent fondue.

I suppose that's it, then.
I do feel peculiar.
But happy.

THE END (AGAIN)

Glossary of Terms

1. The Director: The director is the person ultimately responsible for the film and every aspect of the film. They are the Big Boss and absolutely everyone is trained to serve their vision. This does not mean you can't have ideas of your own, however.

Our director is Susanna White, and she is very good at collaborating with people. The director designs the shapes of the shots and makes suggestions to the actors – well, to everyone really – about what will make the scene work. In a sense, the director carries the whole film about with them all the time, in their head. So that if someone has a specific question about any part of it, the director will be able to answer it. So it is pretty much the most important job and we are very lucky to have Susanna who has directed lots and lots of wonderful things and really knows her onions.

2. The Designer: He or she is responsible for the entire look of the film – the sets and the locations and everything.

3. The Producer: There are lots of different kinds of producers on a film, as you will see, and Lindsay Doran is the main one. This is because she started to work on the film five years ago, which is when I started to write the script.

She edits what I write and sends me about a million pages of notes and then I write it all again. We do this A LOT – it takes years – and then when the script is finally ready, she does the next bit, which is finding the money to make it. Then she and whoever she has found to provide the money choose a director and then things start hotting up.

During the shoot Lindsay is there all day, every day, to solve any problem that arises with the script or actors or – well, anything really. *She* says that she's there purely to help everyone else do their job. That's how she describes producing. It's very hard work and she doesn't get much sleep and she is the best producer I have ever known.

4. The Sound Department: Much as you would expect, this department is responsible for recording all the sounds during the shoot (not the music – that comes later, in the edit).

Simon Hayes is our Head of Sound. He sits at his recording machine and listens like a hawk to everything that comes through the microphones. If there is a noise that interferes with the track, like a plane or some such, he will ask for filming to be stopped until it is quiet. A bad soundtrack means that all the actors have to go into a recording studio after filming is finished and record their voices again. This is called Additional Dialogue Recording (ADR) and it not very popular with most actors because you have to synchronise your lips with the lips on the screen and that's not easy. But Simon and his team are so good that we probably won't have to do any ADR.

5. The Director of Photography (DP): This is the person who is responsible for how the film looks – he or she decides where to put all the lights, what kind of lights they should be, where the camera will work best (although lots of people join in with this kind of decision, especially the director) and what will look good in the frame, which is the bit the camera is pointed at.

Mike Eley is our DP – he is very gentle and peers constantly around, almost like a bird of prey, checking every corner of his frame, checking the level of light, checking the sky if we're outside – he knows everything about the film itself, I mean the black shiny stuff that records the pictures, and he knows everything about the camera and exactly what levels all its little controls should be at. Like the director and the producer, he has to be at work all the time, watching, watching, watching.

6. Other Important Producers: These are the people who have given us the money. It's their job to make sure we a) don't spend more than we have, and b) make a good enough film to see a profit on the money they have given us, and c) support everyone in general.

Eric Fellner and Debra Hayward are our Other Important Producers and they are terrific. They do not have to be there every day, but you can ring them if you have a problem. They are a bit like the headmaster or headmistress who don't necessarily teach you but oversee everyone who does. I hope that makes sense. There are executive producers too and associate producers and sometimes co-producers but they don't often visit the set and you don't really need to know about them.

7. **Set-up:** This means the shot you are working on. One set-up may need many takes. A take is just a go at the shot.

8. **The Camera Loader:** This is the person responsible for putting film away in the right order and bringing new film to the camera and making sure the film is properly protected. It is a very important job. Both our camera loaders, Emma Edwards and Erin Stevens, are trusted implicitly by the camera team to get it right.

9. **The Focus-Puller:** This person must stand by the camera at all times and make sure the film is in focus, i.e. not blurry. You can imagine how important that is. Sometimes they move a little wheel attached to the camera. Sometimes, when the camera is moving about a lot, they move the wheel using a remote control. Our focus-pullers, Russ Ferguson and Matt Poynter, are very experienced, and during the whole four-month shoot there were only one or two moments they found tricky, which is extremely impressive.

10. Animal Trainers and Handlers: These are the people who begin their work months before the film starts shooting – training birds and animals to be ready for their close-ups.

Gary Mui and Guillaume Grange work at Leavesden Studios, which is where they shoot all the Harry Potter films. They bring up birds and animals, sometimes rescue birds, and look after them and work with them. They are passionately devoted to their animals and very proud when things go well – rightly so, because it is extremely difficult to train a bird or animal to do what it is told.

11. The First Assistant Director: Martin Harrison, our 1st AD, must tell everyone what to do all the time. It's not because he's bossy – it's his job. He takes his orders only from the director and everyone else takes their orders from him. He is Scottish and very smiley, so everyone is very happy to do what they're told.

12. The Camera Operator: Phil Sindall is our camera operator on camera A, and Ian Adrian our camera operator on camera B. They look down the eyepiece and actually see what is being filmed at first hand. They are the only people who see this, which makes it vital they understand everything about the scene, the lighting, the frame, the focus and the story.

13. The Dolly: A metal contraption with wheels that you

can sit the camera and the operator on to move it about. The people who work the dollies and move the camera are called grips. I suppose it's because they do a lot of gripping.

14. The Second Assistant Director: The 2nd AD has to listen to the 1st AD and help to carry out his or her instructions. They are in constant communication not only with the 1st but also the 3rd AD and also all the Runners (see below). They must have eyes in the back of their head and know what is going on at all times. Heidi Gower is our Second and I don't think I've ever seen her sitting down.

15. The Dresser: This is the person who looks after everything to do with your costume and makes sure it is all ready for you and helps you to put it on in case there's a zip at the back, like there is in my fat-suit. Needless to say they have to see you with no clothes on and are as a consequence always very discreet, kind people who are good at hiding a shocked expression.

16. A Two-Shot: Oddly enough, this describes any shot that has two people in it. Or two piglets even.

17. Pick Up: This is when we haven't quite managed to finish a scene and we need a few more shots to complete it. These shots are called pick-ups.

18. Singles: A shot of one person. Or one piglet.

19. Props Artists: Our props department is run by Peter Hallam. He and his team must find every single thing that is used by the actors and place it on set. Props is short for properties. It is one of my favourite departments because you can go in and asked for a stuffed owl and no one shrieks 'What??' They just ask you what species.

The props people are on set all the time and they make sure all the right props are there in the right place and the right location. If, for instance, your prop happens to be a hot cup of tea or a squealing piglet, it is up to the props people to make sure your tea is hot and your piglet is squealing. They are wonderful people.

20. Foam Piglets: We had some incredibly realistic stand-in piglets that had to be used in some scenes when the piglets were asleep or under the Scratch-O-Matic. They were very expensive and kept under lock and key by props. We also had white foam stand-ins, which we used for underwater work and throwing about and so forth. The very realistic ones were made of silicone and had thousands of hairs individually punched into their pink skin.

21. Greg: My husband. He is very good at this job and brings me tea every morning and makes comforting noises like 'Not long now' and 'What do you want for dinner?' Also he is not put off by my warts.

22. The Call-Sheet: A piece of paper issued by the producer and ADs every night, which has everything every department needs to know about the next day's filming on it: what we're doing, where we're doing it, who's in the scene, how many cameras, all that stuff. Everyone gets a call-sheet at the end of each day.

McPhee Farmyard Productions

'NANNY MCPHEE RETURNS'

Shepperton Studios
CALL SHEET: 1

DIRECTOR: Susanna White
PRODUCER: Lindsay Doran
Tim Bevan
Eric Fellner
CO-PRODUCER: David Brown

Date: Thursday 7th May 2009

UNIT BASE/ LOCATION: FARM	**CALL: 0800**	
CREW PARKING: As per Unit Base	Minibus 1 depart Security Gate, Shepperton: 0615 Minibus 2 depart Security Gate, Shepperton: 0645	
	B/fast from: Running Lunch from:	0700 (Unit Base) 1230 (On Set)
	Dawn:04:55 Sunset: 20:36	Sunrise: 05:20 Dusk: 20:58

Weather: The day will start with skies grey and by mid morning some patchy rain that's not to stay. After lunch the clouds may clear making way for some sun cheer. Overall a mainly cloudy day and there is really not much more to say.
High 16°C / Low 8°C

UNIT NOTE:
1. Enormous energy & effort has gone into nurturing the flora of this beautiful location. Please be extra vigilant in keeping to demarcated paths & avoid trampling down foliage. It may look like a weed to us, but it's a precious living prop!! If in doubt please consult the 'greensmen' for assistance before embarking on any potentially damaging activity
2. To service this location efficiently it is extremely important to obey the mapped out access system and the instructions of the location/security departments.
3. The very strict 10mph speed limit on location and 20mph on the lane must be adhered to at all times by all vehicles, including gators.

LOC	Scene	SET/SYNOPSIS	D/N	Pgs	CAST
Tilsey Farm	5	INT/EXT COWSHED MEGSIE sweeps up cow dung until the broom breaks	DI	4/8	4,5
Tilsey Farm	14	EXT FARMYARD The squabbling children interrupted by the Rolls' arrival.	DI	5/8	4,5,6,7,8,13
Tilsey Farm	4pt i	EXT GREEN FARM Wide Shot of the run-down Green Farm	DI	1/8	-
		WEATHER COVER SCENES			
Tilsey Farm	6pt i	INT BARN NORMAN disturbs VINCENT operating the Scratch-O-Matic	DI	6/8	4,6
Tilsey Farm	13pt i	INT BARN NORMAN yanks VINCENT off the Scratch-O-Matic	DI	2/8	4,6
Tilsey Farm	56A	INT BARN Disconsolately, CYRIL explores the Scratch-O-Matic	DI	6/8	6,7
Tilsey Farm	19E	INT BARN The Greens & The Grays pelt each other with hay.	DI	1/8	4,5,6,7,8
Tilsey Farm	79	INT BARN VINCENT'S sobbing is interrupted by the little baby elephant.	D	1/8	6
		Total Pages		12/8	

No	ARTISTE	CHARACTER	D/RM	P/UP	ARR	HAIR/M/UP	W/ROBE	L/UP	ON SET
1	ET								
4	Asa Butterfield	NANNY	TR-1	0600	0800	N/A	N/A	-	N/A
5	Lil Woods	NORMAN	2W-1	0750	0830	0830	0850	-	N/A
6	Oscar Steer	MEGSIE	2W-2	0750	0830	0830	0850	-	0915
7	Eros Vlahos	VINCENT	2W-3	0820	0900	0900	0915	-	0915
8	Rosie Taylor-Ritson	CYRIL	2W-4	0750	0830	0830	0915/15	-	0915
		CELIA	2W-5	0750	0830	0830	0915/15	-	As Req
13	Daniel Mays						30		As Req
		BLENKINSOP	3W-1	0700	0900	0930	09/30	-	As Req
									As Req

23. The Line Producer: Another essential producer, who starts work on the actual filming process almost before anyone, doing the budget and seeing how much it's all going to cost and what will be spent on what and then doing a schedule and working out what will be shot when and where. The line producer knows everything about the nuts and bolts of the production. If you need to hire a baby elephant, he's the one who has to go off to Whipsnade, for instance.

24. The Can: This is the camera, really. Well, sort of. It is short for canister, I imagine – the canister in which the film sits, which is also called a mag. But no one ever says, 'It's in the mag.' They only say, 'It's in the can,' which means that whatever it is has been successfully filmed.

25. The Costume Department: As the name suggests, this refers to the people responsible for all the costumes. Sometimes they buy them – for instance, Asa and Oscar are wearing old Aertex shirts which will probably have been bought from a costumes supplier. But my costume and Maggie Gyllenhaal's and Rhys Ifans's have all had to be made from scratch. A lot of sewing goes on, and a lot of washing and ironing. I've got five versions of my costume, because they get smaller as Nanny McPhee gets smaller. Rosie has about ten versions of the costume she gets muddy in – some clean, some very muddy, some torn – all according to what bit of the film we're shooting. It's all a great deal more complicated than it looks.

26. The Script Supervisor: Generally a woman, although I have worked with male script supervisors, this person is responsible for continuity. Continuity means things like when you're drinking a glass of water in a scene, she has to make sure it's always in the right hand and the right place and that the water is at the exact right level for whatever part of the scene you're shooting. If you're in a scene where you're sitting with your legs crossed and you take a break to go for a wee or something, and then you come back and cross your legs the other way by mistake, the continuity person will shout, 'Cross your legs the other way!' Irene never misses a trick.

27. The Video Assist: This is a team of two who tape the proceedings and are able to play whatever has just been shot back to the director. They follow the monitors about with a wee machine – our chief of video is Nick Kenealy and his assistant is my son Tindy, who is always on set garlanded with vast quantities of cabling that he has to keep out of everyone's way.

28. The Sparks: These are the gents who provide the lights and generators. I say gents because I have never in my life come across a female spark. Don't ask me why – I'm as fascinated by light bulbs as the next woman. Paul

Murphy is our chief of sparks (they call him the head of department, also the gaffer, see below) and he works very hard – he and his team lug the lamps about and take their instructions from the director of photography, who is their big boss.

If we're outside and it's windy, you will always see the sparks hanging on to the big lights to stop them from falling over and braining someone. They understand about plugs and electricity and they keep the set safe.

29. The Gaffer: This is the chief of sparks, as described above.

30. The Movement Director: Not every film has a movement director, but we have a lot of tricky action in this film and so have a wonderfully bendy person called Toby Sedgwick, who is teaching the children how to do their own stunts and how to trick the audience into thinking they're doing certain other things, like hitting themselves.

We also have lovely stuntmen (whom I don't have to explain to you, because everyone knows about stuntmen), but Toby designs the complicated scenes. He's a bit like a choreographer, I suppose.

31. The Runners: The name tells you everything. These are young people who look after everything on and off the set and who report to the ADs. They do literally everything and anything they are asked and are often referred to as slaves. We have a remarkable group of runners who will all go on to be other fine components of other film crews. It's a great way to learn about what happens on a film set.

If you want to know the gossip, always ask the runners. They know everything about everyone. Also, and obviously, they run everywhere. That's why they're mostly young (although not usually as young as nine).

32. The Set Photographer: This person must be on set ALL THE TIME to take pictures while we film. These are then used all over the place to publicise the film. It is a very hard job because they have to be almost invisible but they also have to get the best pictures possible. Liam is fantastic at it.

33. The Boom Operator: Boom ops, as they are known, have a very particular skill. They must be able to hold a very, very long pole with a microphone on the end of it for ages. It is really heavy after a while, and you or I would start to shake and wobble and the boom would appear in the picture and everyone would shout at us. Arthur Fenn and Robbie Johnson are our boom ops. Arthur often wears sunglasses as he stays up late a lot – I have never known a boom op like him, because he can squeeze into the tiniest spaces and hold the blinking thing up for what feels like hours.

34. Stunt Double: Someone who is dressed up to look exactly like you but does bits you can't do for yourself, like falling off buildings and things.

35. Second Unit: Second Unit is just a name for another vital camera team that does all the stuff the first camera unit can't manage within the allotted schedule. Mostly stuff that doesn't involve lots of acting, like shots of horses' bottoms.

36. Reading In: This means that if an actor has to leave, someone must read their lines in for the other actors. I do a lot of that because I know the lines quite well after having written and rewritten them for four years (I didn't mean that to sound bitter, by the way).

37. Wrap: The end of the shooting day. When you switch the camera off and everyone is allowed to pack up and go home. The 1st AD shouts, 'Thank you, ladies and gentleman, that's a wrap!' – or 'That's the wrap' or 'It's wrap' or any combination of the above. If you are going to do something like serve a departing actor with drinks, you say, 'Drinks on wrap.' I don't know why it isn't 'at wrap'. It's 'on wrap'. Weird.